The Wall Jumper

THE WALL JUMPER

Translated by Leigh Hafrey

Pantheon Books · New York

A Novel by Peter Schneider

ORIGINALLY PUBLISHED IN THE FEDERAL REPUBLIC OF

GERMANY AS *Der Mauerspringer* BY HERMANN

LUCHTERHAND VERLAG GMBH & CO. COPYRIGHT © 1982 BY

HERMANN LUCHTERHAND VERLAG GMBH & CO. KG

LIBRARY OF CONGRESS CATALOGING IN PUBLICATION DATA

SCHNEIDER, PETER, 1940–

THE WALL JUMPER.

TRANSLATION OF: DER MAUERSPRINGER.

I. TITLE.

PT2680.N37M313   1983   833′.914   83–47749

ISBN 0–394–52928–6

MANUFACTURED IN THE UNITED STATES OF AMERICA

FIRST AMERICAN EDITION

BOOK DESIGN: ELISSA ICHIYASU

The Wall Jumper

1

■ In Berlin, the prevailing winds are from the west. Consequently a traveler coming in by plane has plenty of time to observe the city from above. In order to land against the wind, a plane from the west must cross the city and the wall dividing it three times: initially heading east, the plane enters West Berlin airspace, banks left in a wide arc across the eastern part of the city, and then, coming back from the east, takes the barrier a third time on the approach to Tegel landing strip. Seen from the

3

air, the city appears perfectly homogeneous. Nothing suggests to the stranger that he is nearing a region where two political continents collide.

The overriding impression is of a linear order, one which derives from the rectangle and rules out any bending. In the center of the city, the apartment buildings are massed like fortresses. For the most part they are built in squares enclosing an inner courtyard, each with a chestnut tree in the middle. When the top of one of these chestnuts begins to move gently, residents can assume that a force six to eight gale is sweeping along the streets outside. Berliners commonly call these apartment houses apartment barracks, an expression which accurately conveys the architects' inspiration. And from above, their jagged chimneys awaken memories of the broken glass cemented into backyard walls for protection against the neighbors' cats and children.

The new houses on the edge of the city do not seem to be built from the bottom up. They resemble cement blocks dropped from an American or Soviet military helicopter; even as the plane begins its descent, the stranger still can't distinguish the two parts of the city. While the Eastern countryside was recognizable by the uniform color of the crops and the absence of artificial boundaries between fields, the cityscape offers hardly any guide to political affiliation. At most, the duplication of public landmarks—television tower, convention hall, zoo, city hall, and sports stadium—prefigures a city in which the same taste has brought forth the same things twice.

Among all these rectangles, the wall in its fantastic

zigzag course seems to be the figment of some anarchic imagination. Lit up in the afternoon by the setting sun and lavishly illuminated by floodlights after dark, the wall seems more a civic monument than a border.

On a clear day the traveler can watch the plane's shadow skimming back and forth across the city. He can track the plane closing in on its shadow until it touches down right on top of it. Only when he disembarks does he notice that in this city, the recovered shadow signifies a loss. After the fact, he realizes that only the plane's shadow was free to move between the two parts of the city; and suddenly the plane seems to him a vehicle like those Einstein dreamed of, from which laughably young and unsuspecting travelers emerge to tour a city where, since yesterday, a thousand years have passed.

■ I've lived in this Siamese city for twenty years. Like most of those drawn away from the West German provinces, I came here because I wanted to move to a bigger town, because a girlfriend lives here, because survival in this outpost counts as a kind of alternative service and saves one the years in West German barracks. Like most, I stayed on initially from one year to the next; but the truth is too that after only a short stay in Berlin, all the cities in West Germany struck me as artificial.

I like Berlin, really, for the ways in which it differs from Hamburg, Frankfurt, and Munich: the leftover ruins in which man-high birches and shrubs have struck root; the bullet holes in the sand-gray, blistered facades;

the faded ads, painted on fire walls, which bear witness to cigarette brands and types of schnapps that have long ceased to exist. Sometimes in the afternoon, the face of a person appears over two elbows propped on a cushion in the only window of those walls. It is a face framed by twenty thousand bricks—a Berlin portrait. Berlin traffic lights are smaller, the rooms higher, the elevators older than in West Germany; there are always new cracks in the asphalt, and out of them the past grows luxuriantly. I like Berlin best in August, when the shutters have been rolled down and handwritten signs hang in the shop windows announcing a now hardly plausible return; when the 90,000 dogs are on holiday and the windshield wipers of the few remaining cars clasp sheaves of leaflets for some Live Entertainment; when the chairs stand empty inside open barroom doors, and the two solitary customers no longer raise their heads even if a third one enters.

Only occasionally, when the natives invite me for a Sunday stroll around Grünewaldsee, do I recognize from my unease that I associate these excursions with exercise period in a prison yard. From time to time when a West German visitor remarks on it, I remember something I had almost forgotten, namely that Berliners drive like murderers. They seem in the center of the city to be seized by the need for movement that West German drivers work out on their highways and turnpikes. That same need, it would appear, gives bartenders the steady and apparently limitless growth that their trade alone shows. Now and again, when I see them, I feel irritated by the training crags on the mountain—the only one—constructed from the ruins of the city: a cement block twelve feet high, donated by the German Alpine Association, with every degree of climbing difficulty built into it. Once, when I stopped to watch a rope team outfitted in climbing boots, anoraks, and goggles begin their bold ascent, and then saw the leader at the summit shade his eyes with his hand as he reported the view to the anchor man below, I felt for a moment that I had adapted too well.

But then, when I go on vacation to the Black Forest and a southern German asks me whether I live in East or West Berlin, the price of having all those real mountains seems too high. I've noticed the same ignorance in Dresden or Leipzig; the further you are from the border, the more casually each half-people imagines itself whole. In response to the question of what it is like to live in a city surrounded by concrete and barbed wire, I've long since come to answer like most Berliners: living here is no different from living in any other city. I really don't see the Wall anymore, even if it is the only structure on earth, apart from the Great Wall of China, that can be seen from the moon with the naked eye.

■ A winter night at Schönefeld Airport; it's snowing. Vehicles glide over the field, cast yellow circles of light across the white surface, storm the snow. A tractor digs and shovels, another loads up and carries away, and a third machine, spouting fountains of snow, blows a path free. The field looks like a frozen lake set in a landscape of the future. Only a few automatons have survived here, and are preparing for the arrival of extraterrestrial beings.

An icy wind buffets the arrivals on the gangway; even on the bus it works its way under skirts and up pants legs. For an eternity the driver keeps the doors open in expectation of a passenger lost in the to-and-fro of walkie-talkies. The people waiting come from another part of the globe and another season. Duty-free goods drag at their frozen fingers, their straw hats and kerchiefs offer shelter only from the sun. On the bus there is swearing in Spanish and Russian, silence in German—German lips don't curse the driver. Only when the doors close do Saxon and Berlin accents express relief. But the unity on the bus, certified by a common language, barely lasts for the short run from the plane to the terminal. A gap appears even before the Germans take up positions in front of the two doors marking entry into two different states. A magnetic force emanating from the groups of letters over the doors separates those who, a moment before, stood and walked together; they collect like iron filings around opposite poles. Leather coats part company with vinyl ones, Levis with imitation jeans, natural with synthetic fiber, gaudy with gray. But it's not just the clothes; faces and body motions reveal tribal characteristics, too. Those who group themselves beneath the letters BRD° move carefully and seem to anticipate getting caught in some mistake. In their almost whispered

---

° Bundesrepublik Deutschland (BRD)—German Federal Republic as opposed to Deutsche Demokratische Republik (DDR)—German Democratic Republic. Schönefeld Airport is on the outskirts of East Berlin; Tegel and Tempelhof—mentioned later—are in West Berlin.

exchanges, High German has won out over the dialect. Their gaze seems to turn inward, and the wrinkles around their eyes mark the fatigue of a people whose wishes have come true too soon. The group seeking admission through the other door seems younger, cruder in its gestures, indifferent to strange bystanders. Saxon, Mecklenburg, Berlin dialects clash. Speech demands gesture, and carries hands and shoulders with it.

The two groups conclusively separate as they halt before the two doors: Western faces stare into Eastern faces like men studying apes.

As soon as the rows have formed, all eyes look forward; fingers grip papers, a last token of identity. Elevator quiet spreads among those waiting, and although there is no shortage of air, everyone limits himself to slow and shallow breaths. It is as though they had all reached a doorman who took nothing other than citizenship into account. There is no sound but the buzz of the door opener and then the sliding of the door as it opens and shuts.

With the door closed behind me, I stand blocking the stream of cleared passengers, whose paths now diverge once and for all. Some go right to the Westbound bus, the others left to the parking lot and taxi stand for points East. The terminal is only half-lit, the video monitors no longer show arrivals and departures, the post office is closed, the Siemens pay phone won't take my West German coins. Everyone I ask for change seems to feel he's being watched, and wants nothing to do with my currency. For a long time I walk down the corridors of the terminal building, hoping to find an open exchange bureau, till in the end I hear only the echo of my own footsteps. A man presses his face against a shop window, his profile silhouetted in the glow of a cigarette lighter held up to the glass.

The man turns to me. "You know where Schönhauser Allee?" His accent comes from no language I can designate, except by means of a compass.

"You no Berliner?" he asks.

"Me West Berlin, other side." My native's habit of answering foreigners in pidgin doesn't help us understand each other.

The Pole/Bulgarian/Russian wants to share a cab with me to Schönhauser Allee.

I say, "Me apartment West Berlin, no taxi!" I seize the hand with the lighter and guide it in a westerly direction over the city map hanging in the shop window.

"You there, me here," I say.

To my surprise, the lighter shines on total emptiness. The place I want to call home has no streets, no squares, no subway stations. There are only vacant yellow spaces, relieved by a couple of green oases.

"You living there?" the Pole/Russian/Bulgarian asks, and laughs. "No streets, no houses, everything yellow! Desert!"

"That West Berlin! Berlin: Capitalist, Marlboro, Coca Cola, Mercedes—understand?"

"Ah, you capitalist?"

"No capitalist; I just live there."

"Why no capitalist?" He offers me a cigarette from a pack with a label I've never seen, and takes one of mine.

I notice the big hand on the face of the clock jump across my departure time.

"Me there, you here," I yell, and run toward the exit. But the Pole/Russian/Bulgarian sticks to my heels. Together we stand outside and watch the taillights of my bus disappear in the dark.

"Bus gone, taxi gone, hitchhike," he says.

I nod and point in the two directions at issue. But the man from the East doesn't want to go into the built-up area without me, and he doesn't want to leave me in the desert. After a few steps on the road, he stops.

"Where you go?"

"To Berlin."

"Me too! We taxi together!"

And so we part, stopping over and over again to put down our suitcases and shake our heads, each of us pointing in the other's direction.

■ The Wall is hard to find on a city map in West Berlin. Only a dotted band, delicate pink, divides the city. On a city map in East Berlin, the world ends at the Wall. Beyond the black-bordered, finger-thick dividing line identified in the key as the state border, untenanted geography sets in. That is how the Brandenburg lowlands must have looked at the time of the barbarian invasions. The only reference to the existence of a wall comes under the rubric "Sights": the tourist's attention is drawn to the remains of Berlin's historic city wall, near the old Klosterkirche.

■ When I moved to Berlin, the new Wall had just gone up. Once the initial panic died, the massive structure faded increasingly to a metaphor in the West German consciousness. What on the far side meant an end to freedom of movement, on the near side came to symbolize a detested social order. The view East shrank to a view of the border complex and finally to a group-therapy absorption with the self: for Germans in the West, the Wall became a mirror that told them, day by day, who was the fairest one of all. Whether there was life beyond the death strip soon mattered only to pigeons and cats.

My first forays into the city on the other side awoke no great curiosity. I went to the Berliner Ensemble, paid visits to second and third cousins, had a conversation in a bar in Prenzlauer Berg. Of these first visits I recall little more than a smell, one that I later recognized immediately when I stood on a West German balcony facing the east wind: a smell of fuel mix, disinfectants, hot railroad tracks, mixed vegetables, and railroad terminal.

A friend later took me with him to hear the singer Wolf Biermann. It was during these visits that I first learned of a choice which for me and most of my peers seemed to have been made by birth and our parents' place of residence. Singing his nostalgic and plaintive songs in the apartment on Chausseestrasse was someone who of his own free will had gone to the "better Germany"; and he stood by that address even after no one but his guards and West German visitors were still allowed to listen to him. All his arguments for staying on there referred to a distant past; he himself seemed constantly to reject hopes for the future; and concerning the present, he had nothing but horrors to report. I couldn't figure out what he still liked about the Germany of his choice. In any case, I failed in my attempt to turn his sung and spoken monologues into a conversation. I raised questions and objections with myself in his stairwell, because I hadn't got them out in his kitchen; I rehearsed them for the next visit, which proved just as much a monologue; and finally the unspoken phrases piled up on the steps and blocked my way to him.

On later trips, though, I was amazed by East Berlin. Two conflicting feelings reinforced each other: The half-city beyond the Wall struck me from the start as thoroughly familiar. Not only the garbage cans, the stairwells, the door handles, the radiators, the lampshades, the wallpaper, but even the muted, distrustful life-style over there seemed to me boringly familiar. This was the shadow city, the afterbirth, the emergency edition of West Berlin. Yet, the tendency to recognition was contradicted by the impression of having abruptly landed on another planet. Life there didn't differ simply in outward organization; it obeyed another law. To attribute this to a different social order and pace of development was to label it too hastily. I could orient myself better in New York than in the half-city just a little over three miles from my apartment.

But the inhabitants of the half-city were no longer aware of this other law within a similar life. It remained in force even among those whose "Petition for Release from Citizenship in the DDR" had been answered years ago. In exchanges of political opinion, the difference made itself only slightly felt. It came through more in half-sentences, in a gesture which left something unsaid, a laugh where none was expected, a manner of looking around. Not just ways of talking, but even certain facial lines could be linked to compass points in Germany.

Such impressions were quickly forgotten; yet over the years they accumulated to form a puzzle. It was surprising enough that two antagonistic social systems could have been set up in a span of thirty years and among a people whose spirit was once supposed to "heal the world." That this external antagonism had permeated the behavior and reflexes of each individual in the two systems was even more so.

So long as the puzzle was limited to the Germans on the other side of the Wall, it was only one of many reasons for my visits. But the suspicion that individuals in Germany are in a frightening way interchangeable cannot be discarded at the border. An awareness of individual plasticity in this country doesn't stop at the Wall; and sooner or later, one approaches it in the first person: What would I have become, how would I think, how would I look, *if*?

■ I live on the ground floor of an apartment house that was built around the turn of the century. In those days the part which faced the street, the front part, served as living space for people called gentry; the same was true of the wings. The back part, called the garden house, was designed for the servants, who could tell by a Hammacher & Pätzold Ltd. bell whether they were to wait on the dining-, the living-, or the bedroom. After the second of the Great Wars, democracy, in the form of a dividing wall, took over the apartment houses: the doors between the front and the back apartments were walled up. From then on, income rather than birth and class decided who used the front and who used the back entrance.

The plaster on the building has the sandy gray color that sets the general tone in Berlin; it hasn't been redone in decades. No one can say whether the bullet holes in the back of the building date from World War II or from the street fighting of the twenties. The windows of my rear apartment look onto a small, rectangular garden, which is separated by a six-foot wall from the garden of the neighboring residential fortress. In a chimney-like recess between windowless fire walls stands a maple; it bears leaves only from the fifth floor up, where it catches the sunlight a few hours a day. Flower beds have been marked out with stones along the rear wall of the building. Surprisingly, they sometimes produce flowers and strange bushes whose names no one knows. As a rule, though, the steadily eroding plaster discourages everything except weeds and bushy sumac, whose thin leaves never turn yellow but simply drop just before the first snow. The sumac takes root all over and seems indestructible; in its simple organic structure, maybe even in geologic age, it is the cockroach of the vegetable kingdom.

In both the first and the second inner courtyards, the walls stand so close together that tenants of the lower apartments have to stick their heads out the window to determine the state of the weather. On the other hand, these rear apartments offer a peace and quiet in the midst of the city not to be found anyplace else in the world, not even in the country. This stillness probably ties in with the Germans' habit of hearing their own noise through their neighbors' ears—a consideration which even three-year-olds are taught to show.

Both of the front ground-floor apartments, together with the wings, are leased to bars. One proprietor caters in his cooking and his prices to a public that rides up on bicycles and mopeds; the other to a clientele that has come to expect culinary rather than political excitement from Bolivia. I differentiate the two sets of customers by the marks they leave on my Citroen. The lovers of Latin American cooking put dents in my fenders; the friends of French fries and Schnitzel smash in the side window and rip off my stereo.

The bars haven't changed their cassettes in a decade. I hear the same music whenever I cross the courtyard: on the left, the hollow blowing of a bamboo flute; on the right, the bass guitars of the Rolling Stones. Since I have to skirt the garbage of both establishments on my way to the street, I've never entered either. The difference between German and Latin American cooking becomes trivial when you see the garbage cans. Both cooks fill them with the same tomato cans, moldy green peppers, sprouting potatoes, worm- and maggot-covered cutlets, and yellow and red sauces, which spill out across the courtyard from bursting blue plastic bags.

Once when I found a garbage can filled to the brim with empty cans of cat food, I had hopes of doing in one of the proprietors. There isn't a single cat in the building—the only conclusion to be drawn was that either German meatballs or Bolivian stew had been stretched with cat food. But my attempt to lay a path from the garbage can to one of the kitchens failed: both cooks use the same condiments, and the dill pickle jars and catsup bottles among the cat food cans didn't provide sufficient evidence.

The tenants of my building seldom meet; I know them mostly by their noises. Some of them are so regular I can set my watch by them. Every morning in the apartment overhead, the German hit parade blasts out like a gas oven exploding; then I hear thudding, and the radio is turned down. It took me a while to associate a face with the noise; anyway, I didn't want to meet someone who woke to that crash and started the day with a sprint to the radio alarm. Then one day a baby carriage appeared in the hall, and I hoped the radio alarm might now become superfluous.

Until recently, I could tell it was almost ten by the violin notes wafting across from a window on the upper floors. At first I thought someone shared my preference for certain recordings: Bach's E-flat Partita, Corelli's La Folia, Czerny's Etudes, the slow movement of the Mendelssohn violin concerto. Then I saw a small, very thin man, much too old to be a symphony player, darting between the garbage cans with a black violin case. I saw him maybe four times, and then no more. One day I began to miss his practicing; by the time I asked after the man with the violin case, a hearse had long since taken him away. Since then I've missed that sound among the others—the blaring hit parade in the morning, the moaning of the pigeons, and the pounding of cutlets in the German kitchen that begins punctually at seven in the evening.

The only person in the building who really stands out is a man about seventy who lives directly behind the garbage cans of the Latin American kitchen. His windows give onto the dark inner courtyard; to judge by their number, his apartment consists of a kitchen, one room, and a bathroom. Of all the shadows young and old who pass among the garbage cans, this man cuts by far the brightest figure. I've never seen him other than smartly dressed: he wears a silk scarf over a starched shirt; his face is tanned the year round; and when I say hello, he stops and smiles at me, as though something ought to follow my greeting. Holding himself very erect and not wrinkling his nose, he strides past the garbage cans and ascends the two steps—covered with pigeon droppings—to his door, all with the dignity of someone whose two servants are waiting inside to take his coat and draw him a bath. Once, with his key in the lock, he turned his head and nodded to me as if I were an accomplice in his kindness. I thought I should follow him: behind his door there had to be some secret, a guide to serenity, to a carefree life.

■ It is just a few steps from my apartment to Robert's. Sometimes we meet for breakfast at a café, sometimes for a cup of coffee at his apartment in the afternoon, pretty definitely at Charlie's in the evening. The pinball machine at Charlie's doesn't chirp electronically yet, and when the ball comes toward the flippers, we throw all our weight against the table. The machine reacts as slowly as if it worked by pulleys.

I met Robert in East Berlin, and I knew right away that I wanted him for a friend. I like his quick, strangely persistent gaze and the way he pulls his shoulders up to his ears when he's explaining something. Robert won't talk to just anybody, but when he does speak to you, no one else in the room exists for him. Although he isn't short, he always manages to look at you from below. Occasionally something flares up in his eyes; the grains in his iris shoot apart like fireworks, then regroup around the pupil like a rain of splinters after an explosion.

There aren't any pinball machines in the DDR. At Charlie's, just a couple of months after arriving in the West, Robert showed me the spot on the flipper where you have to catch the ball in order to shoot it off on the most profitable trajectory. He showed me how you catch and slowly let it roll along the flipper to the spot from which the bumpers can be hit. He had figured out how much shoving the machine would take before it penalized the player by flashing TILT. We play either for the next round of drinks or for the next game; the difference is that I play with my hands and Robert with his body, and I usually lose. There are other games, ball games, that I play better, but Robert doesn't like them.

At Charlie's I tell Robert I've begun collecting stories about the divided city.

"Does that really interest you?" he asks. "Who cares about partition besides a few politicians? And they only pretend to, because they want to be elected by people who expect the politicians, at least, to take an interest in the German question."

Robert and I usually talk to each other in the singular. But situations arise in which one or the other lapses into the you-we vein. Robert didn't say "your" German question, but that's how I hear it. The expression "German question" doesn't exist in the DDR, either in official or in daily speech. If Robert uses it, the reason is that he associates my plan with the kind of politicians in the West whom he already didn't trust in the East. His question does, as it happens, give shape to my own doubts. I'm not sure of my purpose in collecting these stories. It isn't the sense of an unbearable situation that has pushed me to the project; rather, my uneasiness at the absence of that sense. The crazy thing is, though, that for all his denial that "the German question" exists, Robert is much more visibly marked by the effects of partition than I am.

After emigrating to the West, he was bombarded with so many questions on the subject that he finally decided not to answer them. It was easy to see that people were interested in him not as a poet who could no longer publish in the DDR, but as a political phenomenon. And Robert had no desire to provide the cheap ego-boost that the West German media try to extract from every emigrant. Since queries about his impressions of the West were usually tied to the hope that he would pledge allegiance to a Western life-style, he preferred instead to hunt for a no-man's-land between the borders. "If it's either Erna or Rita," he would say, "I won't take either; I'd rather jerk off." On the other hand, nothing makes him madder than West Germans' ignorance about their brothers and sisters in the East. Once West German television broadcast an American show on the Holocaust, and the West German chancellor recommended to the chairman of the DDR's state council that East Germany also broadcast the show as a way of atoning for the past. Robert slammed his hand on the table so hard that it bled. "Imagine an ex-Wehrmacht officer," he said, "giving that advice to a veteran of the resistance who spent ten years in a Nazi prison!"

I knew those facts about both politicians, but it wouldn't have occurred to me to link them to the present. I understood Robert's anger; but it was his anger, not mine. Obviously the historical events had different weights in our minds.

Still, Robert rejects any allusion to those differences between us. Nothing else I say can make him quite so mad as the comment that something about him is typically DDR. Probably he knows from experience that the observation of difference often conceals nothing but a mild contempt. Robert counters my readiness to see traces of another social mold in him by stressing the similarities between us. The passage from East to West Berlin probably caused him less strain, he says, than my move from the south German provinces to the Prussian metropolis. After all, he knew the streets, the cry of the newsboy, the haze in the beer hall, the super's glance.

The fact is that after three months in West Berlin, he knew his way around better than I did after three years. He had barely moved into his apartment before he came up with a bar where he could drink on credit. A little later he took me along to a book dealer who gave him discounts; a few months after that, he referred me to his tax expert. He phoned me once from the United States and persuaded me to stop looking at my watch during our conversation: in two days he had gotten the hang of calling toll-free anywhere in the world from America.

All this shows only that we're trapped: I by my tendency to pin Robert to his origins in the DDR; he by his irritated rejection of any allusion to those origins.

■ In conversations with Robert, it has become clearer what I'm looking for: the story of a man who loses himself and starts turning into nobody. By a chain of circumstances still unknown to me, he becomes a boundary-walker between the two German states. Casually at first, he begins making comparisons; as he does so, he imperceptibly contracts a sickness from which inhabitants with a fixed place of residence are shielded by the Wall. In his own person and as though at split-second speed, he lives through the partition process and comes to believe that he has to make a decision, one he had previously been spared by birth and socialization. But the more he crosses from one half of the city to the other, the more absurd the choice seems. Having come to distrust the hastily adopted identity that both states offer him, he feels at home only on the border. And if the philosopher is right when he says a joke is always an epitaph for a feeling that has died, the boundary-walker's story must turn out to be a comedy.

■ One possible name for this man would be Gerhard Schalter, the name of my first landlord in Berlin, whom I lost track of years ago. Until the evening when I visited his apartment, he had struck me only by his Swabian accent ringing out in the stairwell and by a smile which seemed ready for whatever happened. An expectant pleasure always lit up his face, and when I asked him how he was doing, he would look at me as though testing whether I could stand a serious answer.

"You know," he said once, "things are fantastic! Take this morning: I woke up at six and could hardly wait for the day to start. I do exactly the kind of work I like, I get along fine with my bosses, I've got the most amazing people for friends and, as if that weren't enough, I've just found the woman I've been looking for all my life. Every day brings a new, pleasant surprise; and when I go to bed, I can hardly wait until the alarm goes off again. Too bad we have to sleep at all, don't you think?"

The rear exit from Schalter's apartment lay next to the door of my apartment. One evening Schalter rang my bell and asked whether I had had dinner yet. I accepted the invitation and followed him down an endless white

corridor to the Berliner parlor. I was struck by the fact
that such a small man would live in such a huge apartment. Schalter had rented not only the front apartment,
but one whole wing of the building as well. The walls
and doors had been freshly painted, new wiring had
been installed but not yet fully connected, hooks for pictures had been hammered in, and the smell of varnish
still hung in the room. In the parlor stood a drafting
table covered with a white tablecloth; the setting for
two and the candlelight promised a festive and elaborate dinner.

I took the chair Schalter offered, and while he hurried
back down the hall to the kitchen, I sat feeling like a
traveler in a railroad station waiting to meet a wedding
party. The air vibrated with hope; only a loudspeaker
was missing to announce the party's arrival. Schalter
came back with snails and popped the cork on the champagne. As he brought his glass up to mine, I toasted
the guest I was clearly replacing. Schalter didn't waver.
That triumphant smile immediately shaped his mouth,
and if there was a doubt to be read in his eyes, it again
merely addressed the question of whether I could stand
the radiance of his answer.

"Do you know what it's like to look into someone's
face and have your life change completely?" he asked.

In the course of our conversation—more a monologue,
really—it turned out that Schalter had just returned
from Schönefeld Airport. The plane Schalter expected
had landed, but the face he sought wasn't among the
passengers. It was a complicated story. Schalter was expecting a woman married to a German TV correspondent

based in Africa. The agreement was that she would leave her husband in Africa and move into Schalter's apartment with her child. But time and again her departure was postponed. The husband apparently had connections at the highest levels; just one call would make customs officials and airline companies his co-conspirators. Whatever the case, he could prevent his wife's escape; Schalter was convinced that her husband was keeping her caged like an animal, by force and by extortion. Schalter would probably have to go there himself, in order to set his beloved free.

After that dinner I saw Schalter at increasingly distant intervals. Though he still had the inner gleam in his eyes, I no longer asked so carelessly how he was doing. His appearance changed. It wasn't just that he grew a beard or stopped shaving regularly; he didn't seem to care if the sole of his shoe came loose or his shirt split a seam. The pores in his face grew larger, and so did the checks on his shirts. In general, his shirts and shoes made me think that he was digging up the clothes of a relative who had died in the fifties. Wherever he was going during the day, it wasn't the hotel where he worked as an interior decorator—more likely it was Schönefeld Airport.

His trips to East Berlin, which at first had the airport as their goal, evidently drifted from their purpose. His visits to friends he had gradually acquired over there grew more frequent, if only because it was cheaper at the black market rate to call Africa from an Eastern connection. Then he made the discovery that the beer and the food were also more reasonably priced. His visits became overnight ones, and sometimes I wondered, when I didn't see him for awhile, whether he had just stayed in the East. The lower cost of living there made it easier for him to maintain his expensive West Berlin apartment. Almost as a matter of course, Schalter came to see the advantages of the social system in the other part of town. He complained more and more often about the cutthroat competition in the West, about the loss of a sense of solidarity and willing sacrifice. He extolled the DDR's untouched lakes and villages, which reminded him of his childhood in southern Germany, and the women there seemed to him more trustworthy. He spoke with increasingly detailed knowledge about the unbroken power of ex-Nazi officials in the West. My sense grew that Schalter was shifting his exterior and, ultimately, his interior life to the other part of the city. It seemed he came to West Berlin just to get his mail and buy a few presents for his friends in the East.

He appeared bound to the Schöneberg apartment only by a defiant hope, which must have come gradually to seem as hollow to him as the glow of the lights along Kurfürstendamm.

One day a moving van came and took away his things.

■ As long as I've lived in West Berlin, I have treated the structure that is considered a state border over there and a tourist attraction over here as simply an inconvenience. For the first time now, I decide to visit the Wall. I see a tour group climb out of a bus and then take the stairs to a lookout tower. Up top, a few of them put binoculars to their eyes and begin waving. What they see is a tour group on the other side of the Wall just climbing out of a bus run by the same travel agency. They wave back, and people in both groups now train their sights on the watchtower standing between them. What they see there, once they've focused their glasses, are glasses just being focused. Other travelers meanwhile have readied their cameras for shooting. Looking into their viewfinders, they follow the tour leader's finger as he points to an Eastern housefront. There a woman is cleaning windows, a little boy is playing on a balcony, and on another balcony an old man is taking his midday nap. The cameras click. When the woman notices she is being watched, she pauses and stares over from her side. Curious about what she can see from her window, I turn around. I see a man in a grey-green jacket holding a plastic bag in his hand. He wants to cross the street and is waiting until a red Opel has driven by. A woman is waiting on the other side of the street, but not for the man. She is holding a leash in her hand and watching a gray mongrel on the end of it, crouched on its hind legs and straining. Before the man reaches the other side of the street, he stops. I get the impression that he is looking toward the lookout tower from which I'm watching him. I turn back around and follow the tour leader's finger, pointing now at a barely noticeable, grayish-brown rise in the ground. This rise, which hardly deserves to be called a hill, lies in the middle of the prohibited zone and is inaccessible to residents on both sides of the Wall. The leader describes the spot in three foreign tongues, in each of which a German word recurs: *Führerbunker*. The travelers' whispered repetition of the word, the clicking of the camera shutters, the watchtowers all endow the hill with the power of a hallowed place. For a moment the image forms of an armed host to the left and right of their general's command post, sunk in sleep but still waiting for an order.

■ In the evening the television newscaster reports a UN resolution condemning the Soviet invasion of Afghanistan as interference in the internal affairs of the country. On the screen, columns of Russian tanks roll through Afghanistan's capital city. The newscaster says that such footage hasn't been shown in the Eastern media for weeks.

Shortly afterward I switch channels. Again there is a newscaster sitting in front of a map of the world and delivering the news. He is wearing the same tie and the same sports jacket; he has the same receding hairline and speaks the same language as the newscaster on the other channel. He cites a Pravda article condemning the UN resolution as interference in the internal affairs of Afghanistan. The footage is of American and Chinese weapons captured from Afghan soldiers. The newscaster notes that these pictures are not being shown in the Western media.

For a split second, as I turn the television off, I see the shadow of his West channel counterpart; then the screen goes gray.

■ History has taken all the humor out of Karl Marx's ironic phrase, "A specter haunts Germany—the specter of Communism." The specter has settled east of the Elbe, and does in fact look frightful. Political exorcists never tire of assuring us that it remains nothing more than a specter, even though it has grown into a state. Still, they too have long since become used to the sight; now they pretend to be alarmed only on holidays.

When it became clear that the specter couldn't be driven out by the use of quotation marks or the reproachful phrase "so-called" or the pious droning of the Hallstein Doctrine,* the politicians started negotiating with it. The German question has put on weight in thirty years, and you can't claim that Germans west of the Elbe fret over it much. There are people delegated to deal with the question, but they find it increasingly hard to keep their audience alert. It is true that the Constitution mandates resolution of the German question, but the furious parliamentary debates, the struggle over concepts like "re-unification" and "nation" seem artificial. It's like watching the 1,011th performance of a repertory play in which actors and audience both stifle their yawns. The fact that the drama about the sorrows of a divided Germany is still running in Bonn seems less due to anybody's real concern than to tacit understanding that this play has not been staged for the theatergoers at all, but for others who unfortunately can't make it. And besides, what else is there to put on?

* Official doctrine articulated in 1955, whereby the West Germans claimed to be the only valid representative of the whole German people. The doctrine was superseded by Willy Brandt's *Ostpolitik* in 1969.

It would be unwise to conclude, from the frequency of official appeals to the will for unity and the survival of the nation, that the corresponding feelings also survive. A more realistic inference is that most Germans west of the Elbe have long since reconciled themselves to partition. In their separation pangs they resemble a lover grieving not so much for his loved one as for the strong emotion he once felt. In Germany, it seems, time doesn't heal wounds; it kills the sensation of pain.

■ "Your turn," says Robert, after he's diverted the pinball from its path toward the gutter with a deft blow to the table and played it for another 25,000 points. I can't possibly catch up anymore, and I say to the bartender, for whom it's nothing new: "This round's on me."

The only new thing is the drink Robert orders: vodka. Since his arrival in West Berlin, he has tried out several drinks and declared them by turns the only drinkable one. After the whisky period came the sherry era, the sherry era was followed by the cognac season, which after a short and listless gin interlude flowed into the champagne epoch. The champagne epoch seemed definitive. I assumed that vodka, in any case, was completely out.

"Oh, for God's sake, I know what you're thinking again! But it has nothing to do with nostalgia! Vodka is just the all-around best drink. Besides being the healthiest!"

I order a vodka too and tell Robert the story of Gerhard Schalter, my first landlord. Robert listens closely, thinks for a while, orders the next round of vodka and beer, and then asks, without wasting another word on Schalter: "Do you know the story of Kabe and his fifteen jumps?"

■ Mr. Kabe, who was in his mid-forties and on welfare, first came to the attention of the police when, with a running start from the West, he jumped the Wall in mid-Berlin, heading East. Right by the Wall he had discovered a lot where abandoned rubble formed a natural staircase. He could climb it so high that he had only to push himself up by the arms in order to swing onto the Wall. Other reports mention a Volkswagen bus, whose roof Kabe allegedly used for a springboard. It is more likely that he got that idea later, after the authorities had ordered a cleanup operation because of him.

Kabe stood on the top for a while in the searchlights of the Western patrol which hurried to the spot. He ignored the calls of officials trying at the last minute to explain to him which was East and which was West, and then jumped off to the East. The guards of the other German state arrested Kabe as a border violator. Yet even under hours of grilling, Kabe displayed neither political aim nor serious desire to stay on. When asked who had sent him, Kabe replied that he had come for his own sake, that he had simply wanted to get to the other side. He wore out his interrogators, who wanted to know why he hadn't used a border crossing, by pointing out again and again that he lived right across the way and had taken the only direct path over the Wall.

The interrogators could think of no better explanation for this extraordinary reversal in direction than that Kabe had several screws loose. They sent him to the psychiatric clinic at Buch, but the doctors could find nothing wrong with him, other than a pathological desire to overcome the Wall. Kabe enjoyed a special position at the clinic as a blockade runner whose jump had defined the points of the compass anew.

Three months later, a well-fed Kabe was turned over to the permanent delegation of the Federal Republic of Germany. They brought him back to West Berlin in a government Mercedes. There, without showing any emotion, he read the newspaper articles about his jump that a neighbor had collected. Then he shut himself up in his Kreuzberg apartment and remained incommunicado.

The Eastern newspapers sized him up alternately as a "border provocateur" and as "unemployed and desperate." A Western tabloid speculated that Kabe had been paid by the Eastern secret police to jump, so that they could point to one escapee who wasn't visible only from behind. This hypothesis drew fresh support from a journalist who claimed to have traced Kabe from Kreuzberg to Paris. Directly after his return to the West, it seemed, Kabe had taken himself to the French metropolis and, in a suspect part of town, had run up bills which could hardly have been covered by welfare checks.

The truth about this story is that, after three months of free care in the psychiatric clinic in the East, Kabe found three months' worth of welfare payments in his

West Berlin account. In order to fulfill an old desire, he withdrew this sum and bought a ticket on the sleeper to Paris. However, once he had recuperated in Paris at the expense of the two German states, he returned to West Berlin and jumped again.

Brought back once more three months later, Kabe promptly repeated the offense. The West Berlin authorities failed in their attempts to get at Kabe by legal means. After all, he had illegally crossed a state border which doesn't exist in the eyes of the West German regime. In the language of the constitutional law experts, Kabe had merely been exercising his right to freedom of movement.

West Berlin authorities no longer found this interpretation satisfactory, once the East Berlin clinic had presented bills for Kabe's room and board. The West Berliners decided to incarcerate him in Havelhöhe Hospital for self-destructive tendencies. But the diagnosis didn't hold up under scrutiny: after all, Kabe's jumps had proved that the Wall could be crossed going East without damage to body or soul. What's more, they demonstrated that in town, the border strip behind the Wall was not mined. The doctor in charge found nothing wrong with Kabe other than an irresistible urge to overcome the Wall. Rather than a straitjacket, he recommended that the authorities recognize the Wall as a border. They replied that the Federal Republic of Germany couldn't recognize the Wall of Shame as a state boundary just for Kabe's sake. This didn't prevent the doctor from declaring Kabe competent.

Released from the clinic, Kabe went straight back to

the Wall. Altogether he jumped fifteen times and put a serious strain on German-German relations. After one of his last jumps, it occurred to authorities to take him far from Berlin, to quieter areas where he might continue his jumps over old castle walls. He was driven in a government Mercedes to relatives in south Germany, where he behaved very reasonably for two days. On the third day, he bought a train ticket to Berlin and jumped.

Questions about the motives of his jumping drew nothing more from Kabe than this: "Sometimes it's so quiet in the apartment and so gray and cloudy outside and nothing's happening and I think to myself: Hey, let's go jump the Wall again."

■ During the night before the day when I'm to pick up my visa for a longer stay in the DDR, I dream of a boat ride on a mud-brown river whose waters stretch to the horizon. In the stern of the boat, I come upon the vague, somehow blurred figure of a woman. I see her only from behind, but from the contour of her back and the fall of her hair I recognize Lena, with whom I shared the apartment next to Schalter's in Schöneberg. Her presence on the boat seems the fulfillment of an old invitation, too often postponed. I want to speak to her, to express my joy at our taking this voyage of discovery together; but before I can touch the nape of her neck, a wave upsets my balance and I slide overboard. Although the suddenly violent waters keep me level with the stern, my hand can't reach the boat's fender. I swim to shore. Smoke rises among exotic trees, light glows behind win-

dows, human silhouettes become visible; I will not be
lost. But I'll have to find my way through the primeval
forest unarmed; all my personal belongings—money,
papers, clothes—are still on the boat with Lena, sailing
off with her.

I wait until morning and call Lena.

If I have something specific in mind, she wants to
know, could I please say so right away.

"I want to see you."

"What for?" she asks.

"Specifically, because I had a dream about you last
night."

"Well, let me tell you how things look here at the moment"—and she is already counting, Point One, Point
Two, Point Three, all the things she has to take care of
before her imminent departure on a trip. She can find
a minute only if it's something definite, unpostponable,
really concrete.

"Only if you need my help," her answer runs in the
language of our past. But for the present, there is no
urgency and certainly no need of help—at most a trou-
bling desire that has slipped out of a dream and that,
before translation into the language of the waking,
sounds like this: "I'd like to spend a day with you, in
the land which you were the first to show me. And since,
as soon as we speak to each other, we talk ourselves farther and farther apart, I'd like to sleep with you first."

2

■ The platform at Stuttgarter Platz is deserted except for a man who stands clutching the window ledge of a kiosk while he drinks vodka. None of the walls carry advertising, though the German State Railways promises safety on a small poster. Nothing announces a train pulling in but the high, sucking noise I would recognize as the S-Bahn among all the trains in the world. No one gets off. To open the automatic door, I have to force both handles apart like a chest expander.

Silent old people, most of them with artificial leather bags or plastic sacks on their laps, sit scattered among the wooden benches. A young woman in the uniform of the State Railway officials appears at the window and moves her lips into a walkie-talkie. Long, just-washed hair cascades from under her cap. As the train leaves the station, the walls of the houses fall back very briefly, giving a view of the overgrown railroad yard. Bushes run wild among the ties and reach for the coupling of a shunted train car. Then the houses come back again, their windows blind with dust and the curtains behind them like screens hung only to block the view outside. The closer we get to the border of East Berlin, the more the passengers resemble their acquaintances and relatives in that part of the city. The feathers on the pot-like hats, the cut of the coats, the stiff shoes had already struck me in the East group at Schönefeld Airport. Even more telling are the colors: pale gray, olive gray, wine gray, dove gray.

No sooner has the train stopped at Friedrichstrasse Station than a line for schnapps and cigarettes forms at the Intershop kiosk. Even before I reach the steps, I see a fellow passenger holding a plastic bag take a seat on the return train. The border official compares the picture in my passport several times over with the living specimen. He looks me in the face at inexplicable length, focusing not on my eyes but on a spot to one side of my nose. Then he demands to see my ear—not the right one but the left. As I hold my hair up off my ear, I have a vision of Paul Getty, Jr., pulling a severed ear from his jacket pocket and turning it over to the official in an envelope.

As I leave the station building, another time-scheme goes into effect. A holiday is being celebrated, on what occasion I don't know. Red flags are flying from the windows along the main street, little DDR flags stick out of the window boxes on the balconies, a huge construction crane holds the red flag in its claw high over the rooftops. Men in the gray uniform of the worker's militia fill the square in front of the train station. The traveling sign over their heads spells out the news of a state visit by an African revolutionary, who could probably count on being arrested if he were arriving in the other German capital. Children sit on grown-ups' shoulders and wave symbols of state. I know these pictures from Eastern television: the stubbornly closed faces of the parents, raising their arms and waving at the grandstand as though to protect themselves when they feel the camera lens upon them; above their heads, the laughing faces of the children, for whom the state flag is still just a toy. In this foreign country, where the same language is spoken, the fog closes in and blurs the edges of the moment.

■ On another occasion I once stood in this square in front of Friedrichstrasse Station and stared at the traveling headlines as if they could give me a key. That was in another season and another decade. I was accompanying Lena on a visit to her family; she had left them during the days of the Wall's construction and hadn't seen them since. Or was it solely and more significantly the country which she had left and hadn't been able to visit again?

For the first time, then, I sensed a little of the confusion, the falsification of emotions that comes into a family reunion spanning that border. From the greeting to the goodbye, every gesture seemed to me oddly magnified, charged with unspoken hopes or reproaches, strained by an awareness that this might be a onetime event. Though we might have wanted to linger until the next day, the farewell kiss was set by the state for midnight; and to leave ahead of time would have been unforgivable.

The family, meanwhile, had become Lena's homeland. When she laid her head in her sister's lap, I saw a need for peace fulfilled which, in the apartment we shared in West Berlin, I felt I couldn't satisfy. Lena's laughter, which in our apartment always seemed to break out of a memory, rang here with immediacy. The sisters had a shorthand of catchwords, turns of phrase, first stanzas which any People's Army member could have shared, but I never could. It was as though Lena had reclaimed a security which could never content her again, but which she would always miss.

Her family treated her like a daughter whose restlessness confirmed that the price of leaving had been too high. If there was happiness to be had on the far side of the border, certainly Lena hadn't found it. In the family's view, their daughter had returned empty-handed. The mother, whose failing eyesight Lena fretted over in guilty conversations with me, looked at me askance behind her thick glasses and suppressed the question whether I could give her runaway daughter the security she needed. Lena's sister had settled down in the pattern which Lena had found too cramped and bourgeois. She was working as a doctor and raising two children in a country villa. She calmed her doubts about her younger sister's choice of the West with the question: "But it's livable over there too, isn't it?" Everything in her villa radiated warmth and permanence. The pearwood furniture had survived three generations and would fill the grandchildren's apartments; the chandeliers, framed pictures, embroidered covers, upholstered armchairs, and enameled breadbox had outlasted two German empires; the state was powerless before the tiled stove.

By comparison, the state to the West, which claimed to be a society, seemed to me far more violent and powerful, invisible but omnipresent. It had crept in through the cracks in apartment doors, crept into the heads of the inhabitants; it stared at us from bookshelves, stood beside our beds, and filled our dreams with policemen who pursued us.

I believed then that I had grasped something about the origin of Lena's unease. Her need to put down roots didn't involve a man but a society, and wouldn't be satisfied with one individual. It was a need that caused East Germans in West Germany to cluster together, just as Sicilians did in New York City. An inaudible foreign language bound Lena and her two woman friends in the West: they were like three siblings, who rummaged for secondhand jackets and shirts in junk shops, always wore lower heels and less provocative clothes than the native women, spoke more loudly and self-consciously, said "I" more often, used less makeup, and broke into defiant laughter when one of them suddenly recited the first stanza of a Free German Youth song at the top of her lungs.

■ At the taxi stand at Friedrichstrasse Station, the people waiting in line exchange destinations, looking for riders to share a cab. I can't make sense of the street names they call out and get into a taxi by myself, though I have the feeling that this practice is either an archaic custom or one as yet unknown here.

"Always the same thing," the driver responds, to my question about who or what is being celebrated. "The lady with the three initials, who's just turned thirty. Some women only really turn on at thirty, right?"

He watches me in the rearview mirror, as though I owe him a laugh. A banner is being displayed on the roof of a public building. "Stage 30—Duty and Commitment" stands out in white letters against a red background. What stage is that, I want to know.

"The one between Stage 29 and 31."

The taxi driver gets a kick out of baffling me.

"You had your anniversary on May 25th," he says.

"May 25th?"

"The people in Bonn had a champagne party. Don't you read the papers?"

"I do, but I usually skip the ball- and champagne-party coverage."

"I always read the obituaries."

"Do you have that many relatives?"

He laughs. "I'm only interested in obituaries that make the front page."

He checks my reaction again in the rearview mirror.

"Was that a joke?" I ask.

"Why don't *you* tell one?"

"I'd rather not. The only ones that occur to me are East jokes."

"I figured," says the taxi driver. "You've got all sorts of things over there, but nothing to laugh about. No celebrations, no jokes; you have real coffee beans instead. Do you know the one about the fart on the S-Bahn?"

I don't know it.

"Do you want to hear it?"

"No."

I'm puzzled by the bumps in the asphalt that make the car hop at every light. I ask him whether they were laid intentionally to keep people from speeding through the intersections.

"It's the poor asphalt," the driver answers. "In the summertime it piles up under the wheels when the cars brake."

Later I notice that the insignia has been removed from every VW Golf we pass. I reject my first guess—that they were taken off before delivery to eliminate free advertising for the West German company. Maybe amateurs collect them here, the way we do Mercedes stars.

No, I am not an unbiased observer. I suspect motives where there are only material flaws, centralized command in a simple case of collectors' mania. Robert is right; I'll have to watch my passion for seeing things as typical.

■ Pommerer's bell won't ring. The door opens only when I knock. Pommerer rubs the afternoon nap out of his eyes and looks at me as if I were a mistake in his dream.

I follow Pommerer into the apartment. As I look out his eleventh-story window, I hear him putting the kettle on in the kitchen. A boy of about four crouches in front of the television set, watching the Muppets.

"Where are you from?" asks the boy.

Just then the saxophonist of the Muppet Band launches into an incredible solo, which makes the two oldster Muppets in the balcony forget their griping.

"Wilmersdorf," I say.

"Is that over there?"

The boys points out the window.

"Yes."

I'm standing about a hundred feet above street level. The far side of the street is only half built up, and beyond it I can see a stretch of the Wall. On the other side the afternoon sun falls on the metal sheathing of the Springer Building and bathes the facade in a rich golden yellow. Among the high-rises the Wall looks like the decrepit, re-excavated foundation of a building long gone.

"Did you cross the border?"

"Yes."

"What's it like?"

"There's a door at the train station or a barrier across the road, and behind it a policeman is waiting."

"And what does he do?"

"He takes a look at your passport and asks: Weapons? Ammunition? Printed matter? Children? None of the above?"

"Do you have any children?"

"No."

"Why not?"

I pause.

"I know why," says the boy. "It takes two to have children."

■ Later, Pommerer leads me into his study. It lies at the rear of the building, where the view drops through the window to an enormous construction pit. A crane maneuvers close by the window. Beyond it, construction machines are working their joints in the depths of the pit. An apartment tower going up at the right of my view has already come within a floor of Pommerer's apartment and almost hides both steeples of a Dutch brick church. At a fantastic height above the steeples hovers the ballooning middle of the East Berlin television tower; its summit disappears in a cloud.

■ That evening Pommerer and I roam through the barely lit streets. Because of the Wall, what they call Berlin Center is precisely that section of the city where all the side streets are dead ends. It isn't even ten yet, but no one crosses our path. The sound of a motor is so rare that it makes me suspicious.

"Something's missing," I say to Pommerer, "but I don't know what."

"Have you heard this one?" he answers. "A drunk is standing on Leipziger Strasse and grabs a Vopo*: Could you maybe tell me where the hell I am? Berlin Center, the Vopo replies, Leipziger Strasse. No details, please, the drunk jabbers; just which country."

The shop windows are dark; the neon signs have been turned off. In a few high windows of the apartment towers, violet and reddish lights gleam where invisible plants survive the northern climate. At a quick glance these windows look like flares that have gone off and then frozen suddenly into blocks of light against the black sky.

"Anti-imperialist architecture," says Pommerer. "They tore everything down in the fifties here, around Wallstrasse. In those days your newspaper king still ruled the sky and ran headlines around the cornice of his building. You could read Springer's electric news as far away as Alexanderplatz. Our planners did manage to block the view to the West with their apartment towers, but they also wrecked the neighborhood."

"There isn't a mark on the walls," I say. "How do you keep so many surfaces blank?"

"Someone once wrote the word Dubcek with a felt-tip on an advertising column," Pommerer answers. "He made it to the fourth letter—and got eighteen months."

* *Volkspolizist*—policeman.

"Three letters will do it on our side: RAF."*

Pommerer's regular bar is closed, and in the next one they're just turning the chairs onto the tables. We settle for a restaurant named after an Eastern capital, in a new building. My suit jacket gets me by the doorman without challenge. Pommerer's outfit recalls a Western persona that is long out of date: khaki shirt, army surplus jacket, corduroy jeans, shoulder-length hair. But Pommerer knows the waiter.

"How's it going?" Pommerer asks.

"All you have to do is be reasonable," the waiter answers.

"So—two beers, two shots, and a double for you," says Pommerer, and goes on: "Dum dadadum, dadadum. I'm sick of hearing that song. Here we sit in Berlin Center, the Wall is only a few yards off, and beyond it are the all-night cafés of Kreuzberg. But on this side all we get is a lousy song, 'Those Fabulous Kreuzberg Nights—They Never End,' and everything's closed at ten."

At the next table two teenagers are arguing about whether Stevie Wonder cut his first record at fourteen or at seventeen. A blonde waits at the bar for who knows who. She lets her white dress fall around the stool in order to keep the pleats set; the stool legs look like a lamp stand.

"And where's your schnapps?" Pommerer asks the waiter as he sets the glasses down on beer coasters.

"Later," the waiter answers, "later."

---

* Rote Armee Fraktion—Red Army Faction, better known as the Baader-Meinhof gang.

"You just have to be reasonable," says Pommerer.

"Right," says the waiter. "According to Charlie Marx, 'The victory of reason is the victory of the reasonable.' And as Bert Brecht said: 'de omnibus dubitandum est.' Did he even know Latin? Come on, Pommerer, you and I, we've leveled with each other for ten years."

"He always does that," Pommerer explains, while the waiter says his piece two tables over. "He won't drink his schnapps, but he'll put it on the check afterwards. How's your work going?"

My story changes from one day to the next. The only sure thing is that the man whose story I want is caught in a back-and-forth motion over the Wall, like a soccer goalie in an instant replay, always taking the same dive to miss the same ball. Even as I tell Schalter's story to Pommerer, it blends irretrievably with that of Kabe, the wall jumper.

Pommerer listens carefully, thinks a while, orders a second round of vodka and beer, and then asks, without wasting another word on Kabe: "Do you know the story about the three moviegoers?"

■ The house where the group met has supposedly been torn down since. Even now the neighbors are afraid their whole dead-end street will be declared off limits because of the disgrace brought on it by the people who lived at the very end.

It was the zigzag course of the border that put the house in an exposed position. Like a pipeline whose direction people couldn't agree on until the last minute, the Wall headed straight for the house and then veered to the right just short of it. So the building nearly abutted on the concrete mass which, overnight, turned its front door into the back.

At that time two families occupied the house, and two of the three future wall jumpers were just learning to walk. The Wacholt family had the ground floor; the Walz family lived upstairs. Both families owed the survival of their residence to their Party cards and to the fact that they had been among the first to welcome the "anti-fascist bulwark." Since they generally showed a consciousness in keeping with their front-line living conditions, they could be expected to teach their children the difference between a state boundary and a garden wall.

The two sons, who were almost the same age, coincidentally answered to the same name. They knew for sure which Willy was wanted only when one called for the other. This may have contributed to the fact that the two otherwise unremarkable boys developed the habit of listening more closely to each other than to their parents. Besides—as their defense attorney pointed out later—the children's danger naturally increased when Mr. Walz died and Mr. Wacholt moved away to live with his mistress. From then on the Party could not have been adequately represented in the house. But since the two Willys behaved like other children, learned how to jump rope and play soccer, didn't mourn for a paper airplane that flew too far, didn't stand out in political indoctrination classes or in high jumping, their mothers saw no reason to forbid their jumping in the courtyard, the hall, and on the stairs.

Mrs. Walz later reproached herself for not carrying out a plan made by her late husband. He had intended, once the two Willys reached the rebellious stage, to nail down a dormer window in the attic. This window gave access to the roof of a veranda-like porch that served as a tool shed. From the roof, the already short distance between house and state boundary was so abbreviated that a leap from the edge would carry even a middling jumper to the top of the Wall. What's more—as Mrs. Walz might have noticed, had she not been overly trusting—the border guards in the nearby watchtower weren't always strict in their duty. During years of observation the two teenagers discovered loopholes in the surveillance system; in any case, they were reaching the age where they saw only the shortcomings of adults—for example, the fact that a pair of human eyes can't look in two directions at once.

The two Willys learned that guards develop habits on duty. At first the boys only noticed that a man was often alone in the tower and that he shifted his line of sight according to a definite rhythm. They could predict almost to the second when he would show them the back of his head. Then they began to suspect that he didn't notice them even when he was looking in their direction. Experiments on the roof of the porch, starting with a wave of the hand and culminating in a brandished red flag, proved that the roof and the stretch of Wall close to it lay in a blind angle of the view from the tower.

The two Willys might never have made use of their knowledge if the older one hadn't confided in a friend from Prenzlauer Berg. This was Lutz, who spent his life at the movies instead of at work, and who immediately gave the Willys' discovery a practical turn. He screwed a sturdy hook into the ridge of the porch roof, knotted a rope around it, and threw the other end over the Wall. Lutz was the first to leap the narrow chasm between East and West, after which he anchored the descent of the whole rope team from the other side of the Wall.

Once on Western soil, the trio asked for the nearest U-Bahn station and stole a ride to Kurfürstendamm. At the movie house there, they had a choice of *The Schoolgirl Report, Part III*, or *Once upon a Time in the West*. Lutz made a successful case for the Italo-western.

They ran into their first major obstacle at the box office, where the cashier disdainfully hefted their lightweight DDR money. Lutz demanded to see the manager and pointed out that he'd come all the way from Prenzlauer Berg over the Wall to Kurfürstendamm just to watch Charles Bronson. Now, Lutz complained, the cashier wanted to discuss the difference between East marks and West marks. How would he explain that kind of reception to his friends back in the poor part of town?

At first the manager didn't believe the boys' story about their trip from the house behind the Wall to his theater. But when they showed him their identity cards, he accepted them as admission tickets. The six o'clock show had already begun; Lutz knew roughly how the story went, and filled the other two in on what they had missed.

After the show the boys checked the date of the next film—not a real western, Lutz said, but worth seeing because the stars were Brigitte Bardot and Jeanne Moreau. Then they headed home. Barely four hours after their first trip to the movies in the West, the two Willys lay in their beds, and Lutz was racing back to Prenzlauer Berg on his motorcycle.

■ At this point I have to interrupt my story, because the three moviegoers can't possibly have crossed the border in the way I just described.

The border between the two German states, and especially between the two halves of Berlin, is considered the world's most closely guarded and the most difficult to cross. The ring around West Berlin is 102.5 miles in length. Of this, 65.8 miles consist of concrete slabs topped with pipe; another 34 miles is constructed of stamped metal fencing. Two hundred sixty watchtowers stand along the border ring, manned day and night by twice that many border guards. The towers are linked by a tarred military road, which runs within the border strip. To the right and the left of the road, a carefully raked stretch of sand conceals trip wires; flares go off if anything touches them. Should this happen, jeeps stand ready for the border troops, and dogs are stationed at 267 dog runs along the way. Access to the strip from the East is further prevented by an inner wall, which runs parallel to the outer Wall at an irregular distance.

Nail-studded boards randomly scattered at the foot of the inner wall can literally nail a jumper to the ground, spiking him on their 5-inch prongs. It is true that long stretches of the inner wall still consist of the facades of houses situated along the border, but their doors and windows have been bricked up. Underground in the sewers, the border is secured by electrified fences, which grant free passage only to the excretions of both parts of the city.

These facts also struck the experts when the court addressed the matter of the three boys' jumps. Even granting that they could jump the distance from porch to Wall, how did the defendants keep their footing on a surface where even cats slip off? A border crossing seemed conceivable only if a rope had been anchored ahead of time on the Western side—and that presupposed Western accomplices. Lastly, how could the three defendants be sure that they would find this rig still in place on their return? Any passerby with a pocket knife could have severed the umbilical cord linking them to socialist life.

But as the defense attorney pointed out, everyone knows that even the outer Wall stands within DDR territory, in order to leave room for painting and repair work. Even if a rope had hung down on the west side, Western citizens would have considered it untouchable. In addition, the defendants had made their jumps when the "modern border"—as it is called to distinguish it from the old, single Wall—wasn't complete. The inner wall still had weak points, while the outer Wall was often a brick structure flat on top instead of round.

These arguments did not allay skepticism about the boys' improbably aerial route; the suspicion was that they had found some underground passageway to the West which might still be serving a band of successors. The means that Lutz and the two Willys did in fact use to make it over and back have vanished in the wilderness of oral transmission. Technical difficulties that seemed insurmountable were resolved in the imagination of those who spread the story. The remarkable thing about it, after all, was not that the trio found a way to the West, but that they traveled the route in both directions.

As casually as other DDR citizens drive out to Müggelsee on a Sunday, Lutz and the two Willys went to the movies on Kurfürstendamm every Friday. Moreover, they always went to the same theater at the same time. Though they soon knew their way in the dark, they preferred to go in the afternoon rather than risk finding a sell-out at the evening show. Sometimes they took a break when a film went into its fifth or eighth week and wasn't worth seeing again. And so, within half a year, they gained a complete overview of programming at the last Cinemascope theater on Kurfürstendamm.

In all, the trio jumped twelve times. Their achievement first came to light in a story by a West Berlin journalist. On the day they crossed over to see Marlon Brando in *Queimada!* they were stopped by a West Berlin patrol. Lutz denied that they were refugees; he presented himself and the two Willys as fans of westerns. That, and the fact that the three refused point-blank to stay on in the West, struck the policemen as so incredible that they phoned the city desk of their favorite newspaper. A reporter caught the trio that day as they were leaving the theater and loosened their tongues with curried sausage and whisky.

The newspaper story put the State Security Service on the boys' trail. The two Willys were arrested at their desks in school and brought to court for repeated violation of the passport law and illegal border crossing. The defense based its case on the unquestionable patriotism of the defendants. After all, they had had a dozen opportunities to leave the DDR and hadn't taken them—a proof of loyalty that few DDR citizens could match.

This defense was rejected and the boys were found guilty. The older Willy was taken out of school and thrown into the army; the younger one was sent to a youth work camp. Lutz—who had turned eighteen and was subject to the full weight of the law—escaped imprisonment owing to his passion for movies. On the evening of the trio's last excursion, Lutz had returned promptly to his favorite neighborhood movie house in Prenzlauer Berg for a showing of *High Noon*. He had been standing in line a quarter of an hour when the projectionist announced that the show was canceled— the film had torn. At that moment Lutz felt that something inside him had torn too. "You run your heels off from Kurfürstendamm to Prenzlauer Berg to be on time . . . and then the film is torn," he snarled at his neighbor. "That does it!"

Lutz stepped on his motorcycle's starter, raced at top speed back to the Wall, and hurried through the darkness into the West, in order at least to catch the late show of *The Big Country*. It was his last transit. In the

West he became what he had always wanted to be in the East: a lumberjack. But since he knew the West only from American and Italian westerns, he was poorly prepared for logging in Western woods. To this day he can't understand why a lumberjack should have to buy his own ax and saw.

■ The waning moon stands behind the spire of the television tower, changing it into a Turkish minaret for the rest of the night.

"Do you hear?" says Pommerer, and stops walking.

A rumbling sound approaches under our feet, swells to a thumping and banging as though an elevator were falling down its shaft, then ebbs.

"Line 6—it runs right under my former apartment. You know those sealed-off stations down there? I never wanted to go to the West. But sometimes, when the teaspoons in the kitchen started vibrating, I'd think: Just once I'd like to be sitting in that train and riding on through."

It isn't midnight yet when we reach Pommerer's place; but when I open the door to his study, it's as though I've come to the wrong apartment in my vodka haze. Blue lightning streaks through the room; the table, the chair, the bed, the books dance in a shower of sparks. In the course of the evening, one wing of the new building by the window has grown another story. Two workers kneel on the cement floor and solder iron parts.

"To the West they gild, in the East we build," says Pommerer, and wishes me good night.

■ The next morning I go to the department store across the street and ask for the stationery section. I purchase a notebook for 84 pfennigs and return to sit down with it at Pommerer's desk. Since last night the inexorably growing high-rise has blocked my view of the television tower. The crane swings close by the window; now and again, the screeching of winches and the squealing of the crane are punctuated by yelled half-sentences that fly back and forth between the operator and the workers in the pit. I watch the operator execute a half-turn that brings him face to face with me. We are now on the same level, and we light cigarettes at almost the same time.

I'm not sure whether he can make me out behind the windowpane; but then, as though to ape me, he leans on his elbow and digs his chin into his fist. We both hold this posture briefly and look at each other, alike for a few seconds in the midst of such unlike occupations.

My notebook has a green, blotter-like cover. I leave the lines for name and title blank and write the date on the first page. I will have to start fresh here on the story I left behind in the other part of the city.

■ I imagine a day on which two factors combine: a fog has settled on the backyards of Kreuzberg, and a new show has started its run on Kurfürstendamm. At about five in the afternoon on that day, Mr. Kabe leaves his apartment in Kreuzberg, and Lutz leaps on his motor-cycle in Prenzlauer Berg. Both of them—Kabe on foot and Lutz at a felonious speed—head in opposite directions straight for the Wall. At about the time that Kabe reaches his usual spot at the Wall, Lutz kicks his motorcycle up on its stand in front of his friends' house and with one name calls both their heads to the window.

As Kabe begins his run, he notices that his launching pad has been abbreviated: by order of the Senate, the heap of rubble has been removed since his fourteenth jump. Kabe walks along the Wall in search of another route. He discovers the rope across the border just as his counterparts on the other side are crawling out the dormer window. Kabe hauls himself up the rope and is getting set for his fifteenth jump, when Lutz and the two Willys launch into their twelfth. The fog is so thick that Kabe ducks Lutz, who is jumping blind, without a second to spare. The two involuntarily embrace in order not to fall off the Wall on the wrong side—West for Kabe, East for Lutz. A few seconds later the two Willys land beside them.

Then, I imagine, all four introduce themselves as pros and take time out for a short exchange of views in the blind angle of the watchtower. What would the Eastern jumping collective and Kabe the lone jumper say about their motives?

Probably Lutz and the two Willys would simply mention *Queimada!* Probably Kabe would extol the food and good treatment at Buch Clinic. But any discussion of reasons for jumping wouldn't last long; it could hardly be more interesting than the exchange between two rope teams who meet unexpectedly on K2 and give the nice view as a reason for risking their lives. If Kabe and his counterparts talked about anything, it would probably be the technical difficulties of their sport: weather conditions, ascent routes, climbing gear, intermediate camps. Perhaps the four of them would even pay homage to some of the pioneers who conquered the Wall long before them, often by more difficult routes. After all, in the early sixties a circus acrobat had used a high-tension wire as a tightrope to walk into the West. And hadn't a pole-vaulting champion used the Wall as a bar and cleared it with room to spare? There was no end to the list, and on the basis of sheer imagination, it would be difficult to select candidates for a hall of fame.

The suppression in the DDR of sports that might lead to border crossing—ballooning and scuba-diving, for instance—had loosed a tide of fantasy and produced a generation of inventors. Snorkels, diving masks, and oxygen tanks had hardly disappeared from the stores before hobbyists of all kinds began fashioning replacements out of bicycle inner tubes, home heating gas containers, and rubber aprons. Where in a hall of fame would one place the auto mechanic who developed a miniature motor to pull him across the Baltic under water? And how would one rank the engineer who, after searching the specialty bookstores in vain for textbooks on aerodynamics, rediscovered the principle of the hot air balloon?

The one sure thing—and here the dialogue on the Wall could take a philosophic turn—was that every improvement in the border system had spurred the creative drive to find a new loophole. The urge to master the Wall didn't differ in substance, perhaps, from the impulse to climb K2: the Wall, like the mountain, was there; and the challenge would persist as long as the Wall remained standing.

■ I stand at the window with Pommerer's telescope. A border guard is raking the sand in front of the Wall. Over to the right, his colleague sits in the observation tower and watches him work.

"Sure you can get over the Wall, even here in Berlin Center," Pommerer says. "You can see that the strip isn't mined in town. Those guys rake the sand every evening, so they can follow the tracks left by any trespasser—man or beast—the next morning. Otherwise there are only trip wires, and sometimes no one's even in the observation tower."

"How do you know all this?"

"I've checked out every inch with my telescope."

"But you said yourself you didn't want . . ."

"And I don't. But when you've got a thing like that staring you in the face, finding the flaw becomes an obsession."

"And have you found it?"

"I think so."

■ It's Sunday, the streets are empty, the countryside lies flat under an unmoving sky. The gray of the cloud cover is so solid, you'd think it was the sky's permanent color. When I turn around in Pommerer's car, the skyline looks like an ice-capped mountain ridge, radiating cold far down into the plain. The landscape seems numbed; every leaf, every twig on the trees by the roadside is covered with a white powder. The tips of the fence posts, the transmission lines look as though they were coated with a permanent hoarfrost—a landscape that can't breathe.

"A lime factory nearby," Pommerer explains. "It buries everything in dust for six miles around."

Later we drive through summer greenery. Time and again water gleams behind the roadside bushes. It reflects neither house nor sailboat, only treetops. As we speed past the shrubs and lakes, I am overcome with amazement, as I was once on a trip from New York to Philadelphia. It wasn't right, I thought then, for the same spruces and maples to grow on both sides of the Atlantic; the grass shouldn't be the same color; the lake shores shouldn't have the same vegetation.

Most of the houses in the villages and towns we pass through have one, at most two stories; the churches are still the tallest buildings. Here, the banners that are posted everywhere assume an air of exhortation: in the display window of a shoe store, it says, FIGHT TOGETHER, WIN TOGETHER; on the facade of a town hall, SOCIAL SE-CURITY, HUMAN RIGHTS IN ACTION; outside a restaurant, HAPPY PEOPLE, PROUD ACHIEVEMENTS, STRONG REPUBLIC; in a fish store, 30TH ANNIVERSARY, OUR CONTRIBUTION— pinned up between a Baltic eel and some canned mackerel. A few of the posted aspirations read like threats: SOVIET UNION—FRIENDS FOREVER. And one, IT WILL AL-WAYS BE OCTOBER, has a kind of involuntary melancholy.

So many people must question what these slogans say, to repeat them so anxiously.

Some years ago, it struck me as my plane from the West was landing that the usual announcement over the PA system—"We have just safely touched down at Berlin-Tempelhof"—had skipped a word. Overnight, it seemed to me, the qualifier "safely" had been stricken, presumably by the airline's PR department because it implied the possibility of an unsafe landing. Western public relations experts know that it's smarter to pass up the self-praise.

A comment Pommerer made during our drive through the dusty landscape takes hold and echoes in my head like a password, a rule for survival: "You should see this sometime when the sun is shining."

A gravel path leads to a group of abandoned farm cottages, where some friends of Pommerer's have settled. Deer at the forest's edge, a stork's nest, barking dogs, endless fields separated by natural boundaries—a stream, a pond, a clump of trees. Only the enormous TV antenna on the roof of one of the larger houses evokes a different frame of reference, an invisible life that is tracked from this receiving station.

We sit over coffee and homemade cake; high-proof alcohol from the Intershop stands on the kitchen table; smoke from Western cigarettes hangs in the air. The kitchen fills slowly with neighbors who take ostentatiously casual notice of the Western guest, as though they don't want to admit their curiosity. Conversation focuses on the daily life of this group of artists living in the country: finishing an attic, fixing a muffler, extending a lease. Arguments start up about art and literature; politics is allowed only in the form of cunning phrases and is accompanied by Jimi Hendrix records played loud.

"I suppose you get Radio Yerevan with that giant antenna of yours," someone says to the host.

"Peking, when the weather's good."

One of the neighbors turns to me. "Hey, don't you think you could put up an antenna in the West that would cover the whole DDR? If you don't, our host here is going to build a replica of the Berlin Broadcasting Tower right here."

"Why bother?" someone else says. "The sheep will be happiest if they can't hear the West."

"But if everyone is happy, the Stasi* will be out of work."

"In that case, let's all have Western TV!"

"Your attention, please! At 15:02, Author X publishes a call for the erection of a television tower capable of reaching the whole DDR."

"Jimi Hendrix said that. I only play the music here."

"Don't kid yourself—pop and agitprop are all the same to them! But okay: At 15:02, accompanied by Author X on the bass guitar, Jimi Hendrix calls for the extension of all Western radio and television antennae."

"Say it again, so they'll hear you."

"They hear me, all right. You know the Russian formula for concrete: a third cement, a third sand, a third microphone."

---

* Staatssicherheitsdienst—State Security Service.

"Ouch! Now I know why my tooth hurts. They put too much microphone in the filling."

The distinction between friend and foe seems simpler here than in the West. The myth of the omnipresent ear of the State, even when they refer to it ironically, holds the group together and gives their exchanges the charm of a conspiracy, even though the conspirators are in fact devoted only to the arts. The unpublished or difficult writer is accepted by the group if he is involved in a visible struggle with Party or publishers. The successful writer, especially someone who has won a State award, meets with distrust.

After a while the conversation narrows to two topics: the approval or refusal of a travel permit to the West, the approval or refusal of publication. Someone is working with his editor on a new novel. The editor has okayed publication, but is bothered by certain words that appear "too often" in the text. The word "police," for example, needn't be altogether eliminated, but it doesn't have to come up six times—twice is enough. The editor doesn't like the last word in the phrase "order to fire," and he doesn't like the word "conformity" at all. Another writer who has just returned from the U.S.A. passes around a photocopy of a newspaper clipping. Under the heading "Correction," the American paper reports a typo in an interview with this writer: he did not say that the October Revolution was a "monstrous event." The statement should have read: "monumental event." The writer carries the clipping around with his ID card—a warranty for his next trip to the West.

A third writer joins in: one of his novels contained a

sort of documentary description of assembly-line work in a textile mill. His editor complained that the passage was too much like a Wallraff exposé on piecework in Western companies. "But I didn't copy it; I saw it with my own eyes," the author protested. The editor agreed to give the section another reading, but after a while the author got his manuscript back with the passage marked "distorted vision."

Another story: A photographer is summoned to the executive offices of her periodical. She finds the photos from her last few articles hanging on the walls of the office, numbered and arranged in order, and she knows she is going to have to justify herself.

The executive editor points to a series on pitwork in a mine. "You focus repeatedly on the gray, the dismal side of the socialist working day. Almost as though the sun never shone here."

"But I was down there myself," the photographer answers. "I shot what I saw. And I feel—"

"What you feel doesn't matter," the editor breaks in. "It's a question of what we make others feel!"

The Western guest keeps silent, shocked by these tales. He has nothing comparable to offer. To show surprise, let alone anger, would seem a waste of emotion, a luxury of sentiment on his part. And he would only be revealing his naïveté if he shouted what he has been thinking: Why do you put up with this, even for a day? Get out; you can do it! Either go or stay; there's nothing in between—there's no point to this joking tone, these token trips approved for a few dozen state-subsidized dissidents!

Later in the conversation, my counterparts are just as surprised as I am when a scientist who has joined the group tells us that he can't travel anymore. On his last trip to the West, he explains, he broke nearly every clause in his travel directive.

"Travel directive—what's that?" everyone asks.

It seems that this set of regulations, which doesn't apply to writers, forbids any contact with relatives or friends in the West, any unauthorized straying from the site of the congress, any interviews, any statements.

"And because you didn't stick to that, they won't let you out again?" the writers ask the scientist. "That's incredible!"

Honor the wisdom of the Stasi! By treating each group differently, it embroils them in maintaining their own privileges. The norm vanishes in the process. Every group develops a strategy of limited and reasonable risk. Those who don't abide by it have only themselves to blame for the consequences. So the group comes to distrust people who push too far and wind up in jail or stripped of their civil rights just as much as it distrusts national prize-winners.

I saw this mechanism at work for the first time when Wolf Biermann lost his civil rights. No one had harsher words for Biermann than those who protested against his exile. They couldn't forgive him for ignoring the group consensus on limited risk. The accusation that he had knowingly provoked the state by his performance in Cologne was justified by the logic of group consensus: Biermann had challenged the state instead of outsmarting it, so he shouldn't be surprised at the consequences.

But the accusation also expressed the group's hatred of an individual who doesn't stick to its rules for survival: he reminds the others that they may have put up with tyranny too long and too cleverly.

Towards evening I grow increasingly restless faced with the unrelenting greenery, the storks and the deer, the ticking wall clocks, the incessant chewing and gulping, the conversations about wrangles with publishing houses and Party bureaucracy, the hair-raising tolerance for these petty struggles. Every story is told three times over, because more guests keep arriving. I sit stuffed and embarrassed, fighting boredom and a guilty conscience.

You should see this sometime when the sun is shining.

■ Back in Berlin, Pommerer receives another visitor from the West. We've hardly said hello when his friend plunks down a carton of Gauloises and a plastic bag containing the minimum sum she was required to exchange at the border. I already know this woman with the round face and slightly bulging eyeballs from encounters in West Berlin. Every committee that has the word "solidarity" in its title puts her at the top of the mailing list. If a human right is trampled on anywhere in the world, she seems to come out of it with bruises of her own. She always talks as though she had just outrun a hundred policemen; her face bears the mark of others' grief.

In Pommerer's apartment she seems more relaxed than I've ever known her in West Berlin. In the East, it appears, she can recover from the rigors of the struggle in the West. Here at last she has sympathetic listeners; here she can catch her breath. But this is a delicate balance: Eastern tales of woe would upset her sense of having come from the worst of all possible worlds. The idea that she enjoys certain freedoms in the West—if only freedom of movement—would weigh unbearably on her conscience. She can't afford to admit that she has any privileges, because she derives her identity from her status as victim.

As a result she tries to override any reference to limitations on life in the East by telling horror stories from the West. She immediately parries the story of an unknown DDR writer, jailed for signing a petition to the government, with the case history of someone who has been excluded from his profession. If the conversation turns to food shortages in the East, she cites figures on the unemployed back home, who see oranges in shop windows and can't buy them. There may be more housing in the West, but no one can afford it. True, it can take as long as twelve years to receive delivery on a car in the East, but the cars you get so easily in the West clog traffic and pollute the cities. Granted that you can voice criticism in the West, but it has absolutely no effect. And in the final analysis, the repression of dissident writers in the East proves that they're taken seriously.

I already know, and try to avoid, this conversational rite in which the progressive visitor from the West attempts to reconcile his Eastern friend to his situation by showing him that things are even worse in the West. Unlike the Western media, he sees it as his role to destroy every illusion about the West. Yet he proves like the media in a crucial way: the urge to compare distorts his view of his own society as well as of the foreign one. Every observation is invalidated by the reflexive search for a correspondence on the other side of the Wall. What matters is whether people with whom you wouldn't want to be identified might make the same observation, not whether it's true. Equivalence substitutes for perception, and reduces the act of listening to a defensive nod just before the rebuttal.

A friend of Pommerer's once said, "It's remarkable how some people who come to visit us talk about nothing but abuses in the West—when we'd be so happy to go over and take a look at their abuses!"

I am all the more amazed now to see Pommerer hear his Western friend's confession with some satisfaction. She evidently meets a need I haven't fulfilled, haven't even noticed. So far, I've tried to take the stance of a foreigner with nothing but his senses to depend on.

At first Pommerer was curious about the responses my foreign gaze on his surroundings would elicit. Since then, his curiosity has increasingly given way to the need to protect his routine from the impudence, even the stupidity of my first impressions. I am shocked by certain restrictions on his life which he has long since accepted. My shock inescapably reminds him of his initial feelings, which he has rejected as pointless. More and more often, he counters my reactions by referring to parallel phenomena in the West.

A couple of days ago, for example, he found a document in his mailbox that had been sent out by something called the Commission on Order and Security. The form, already inscribed with the tenant's name and apartment number, calls upon him to "report any infringements of order, cleanliness, and police registration requirements you may observe within your housing community. Relevant communications should be addressed to the Housing Community Section Supervisor."

Pommerer quashes my outrage at this enforced squealing. "And what about your Neighborhood Association? A friend of mine was evicted recently from his apartment in Charlottenburg. The Association official was tipped off by the landlord, and found out that my friend was letting a woman live in his place without a sublease. Has it ever occurred to you to compare that friendly old man with his walkie-talkie to a Nazi block warden?"

A section supervisor is not the same as an association official is not the same as a block warden. We can fight the infection as much as we like, but Pommerer and I have long since contracted the disease of comparison.

■ The evening news: DDR-TV starts with documentary footage of an offensive launched by a Central American liberation movement. The work force in 40 factories has heeded the call for a general strike, 800 soldiers from one camp have deserted to the rebels; contrary to all denials by the U.S. government, counterinsurgency units are being trained at and supported from at least four U.S. military bases. As his source the commentator cites the liberation movement's radio station, "Liberación."

Half an hour later, the Western channel's newscaster reads a bulletin on the same offensive. The strike call has had little effect in the capital, work has proceeded as usual in all the large factories, only a few stores on the outskirts of the city have closed; government troops claim advances against the guerillas. As his source the commentator cites a statement by the ruling junta.

Probably both broadcasts are true. The liberation movement's strike call has been widely followed in the countryside, but in the capital city, fear of the death squads and government troops has defeated it. Two views of a struggle in a distant land: each German broadcast releases for consumption only that part of the event which the station executives want to believe is true.

"Practically speaking, not much has changed on your side," Pommerer says. "It's the same old powers, done up as a democracy and allied with the reactionaries of the whole world. On our side, at least, class relations have been turned around for once. Most of the DDR people in power come from poor families, and so do the leaders of the intellectual opposition. They are real sons of the working class. What do you have that compares?"

"But," I answer, "your arguments—reversing class relationships, building an anti-fascist state, supporting progressive forces in the Third World—all refer to the past or to circumstances out there, beyond the Wall. Your line about a better Germany—always depends on the past, never on the here and now."

"It took centuries to develop capitalist democracy," Pommerer retorts. "Why should we expect socialism to mature in a couple of decades?"

■ There it is again, the canned language, the state grammar, the lesson dutifully learned. No, I'm not just some
foreigner, come with nothing but a suitcase and his five
senses. The foreign country I come from is called the
Federal Republic of Germany and my views, like Pommerer's, are predetermined by a half-country that over
thirty years has acquired an identity in opposition to
its other half. What would happen if, say, both German
governments took a year's vacation; if the journalists fell
silent for a year; if the border police took a year to re-
cuperate on the Adriatic and the Black Sea, and the
people started their own East-West negotiations? After
a brief embrace, they would discover that they resemble
their governments much more closely than they care
to admit. It would become evident that they have long
since made their own crusade out of the biographical
accident of growing up in different occupation zones—
later, different social systems. As soon as someone asked
which half offers a better life, the fight that both states
carry on daily in the media would break out in the living
room. Those who until then had acted as bystanders
would be forced to recognize their own crudely ampli-
fied shadows in the two-dimensional figures on TV.

■ Free jazz at the "Hall of Young Talent": that's what
they now call a mansion that once served as a town
house to members of the Prussian royal family. Seated
around a rectangular stage with glasses of orange soda
or red wine in their hands, some two hundred teenagers
listen, curiously erect, to the inferno of sound unleashed

by six musicians. No emotion, neither approval nor ob- jection, shows in those faces, only a wondering, unbroken concentration. The musicians guide their instruments through a carefully laid-out labyrinth of sound, until they reach an expressive limit at which the keyboard hammers, bass strings, saxophone stops, and drumsticks seem to go up in a blinding flash. The breaking of all prescribed tonal systems, rhythms, and harmonics comes across in the closed room as a promise, a rebellion that can't be put into words and, therefore, can't be censored. As the last drum roll fades, a brief burst of applause runs through the room; the musicians take a bow, crisp, al- most military, and pack up their instruments.

Afterwards Pommerer walks with me through the night-dark streets to Friedrichstrasse Station, a short dis- tance away. He stops suddenly in front of a construction site and points with triumph to a black spot on the fence.

"They actually got to five letters!" he whispers. "Five letters!"

I stare at the black rectangle, which gradually takes on shape in the glow of a construction lantern. Beneath the coat which someone has laid on with a broad brush, I can see a paler background; I make out the ends of letters at the upper and lower edges of the rectangle.

"And what did it say?" I ask.

"Five letters!" Pommerer repeats. "Doesn't that tell you anything?"

I recite some names to myself and count the letters: Lenin, Bahro, Brecht, Brasch; there are a lot to choose from.

Later I stand in line with Pommerer at the gate marked Citizens of the Federal Republic of Germany— West Berlin. It is two minutes to midnight. As the second hand jumps toward twelve, a southern heartiness wells up briefly in the crowd: embraces, tears, kisses. Those who are staying behind wait until those leaving turn their backs definitively.

"See you in a couple of days," Pommerer yells, and disappears behind the waving arms.

"Good evening," I say to the border official, who is silently looking at my ear.

"Good morning," he sets me straight after a glance at the clock. It is indeed two minutes after midnight.

3

■ At the sight of the broad taillights on the cars, the faint glow of the display windows, the Mercedes star rotating atop the Europacenter, I am gripped by the same impulse that seizes drivers after one hundred and twenty miles on the transit corridor from West Germany to West Berlin: I want to step on the gas, let off steam. I want to order a beer again after midnight, buy a paper, hold a handwritten menu in my hand, look into a decadent Western face, wait for the dawn in the hum of voices and song. These pleasures turned hollow long ago, but the fact of having done without them for a while makes them irresistible again.

The familiar faces gathered around the bar turn toward a new arrival with a spent, hopeless look. The only live presence is Esther, the woman behind the counter. She knows the drinking habits, debts, and love affairs of her paying minions and keeps an eye on every movement in the room.

"It's quite a story!" she says to me, and grabs another customer by the coattail. "Pay up before you go!—So Bill came up to bed while I was at it with Marlow. Let's get this straight, he says, one of us is going to have to disappear. It had to be Bill, naturally, or I'd have gone crazy on the spot—Can't you pour the sherry yourself, Katt? No, there's no more pear, let him drink plum, he can't tell the difference at this point, anyway."

She fetches a bowl of goulash soup from the kitchen at the end of the counter, and goes on with her story from there while she tucks bread and utensils onto the soup plate.

"So Bill did in fact leave, but that Marlow's a lot more sensitive than he looks, he's incredibly open and sweet, he was popular here by the third day. And so he says he can't fuck under pressure, with Bill outside the door he just can't do it . . . me neither, actually—Three vodkas, two beers; hold it, there was a third one here, who's paying for it? Anyway, I called Bill up an hour later, and he said I should come right over!—What do you mean, too slow? Look, guys, can't you see I'm busy!—So

I went over there in the rain, Bill gave me grief for three days straight, and by then Marlow was back with his rock group in Milan. Was it dumb of me to decide in such a hurry? Should I have dumped Bill for that black comet? He's an ass, Bill, but I've know him for three years now."

A bit of mascara has caught in her long lashes, and while she is smoothing it out with her fingers, she laughs and shoots me a mocking glance out of the other eye. Then she grows stern as she reminds a customer of the shots he's forgotten to mention.

Later I sit at the bar next to the impresario of some Berlin festival. When I tell him where I've just been, he looks at me as I were a traveler back from safari.

"Can you go over that easily?" he asks. He has me explain how to apply for a visa, when and where you pick it up, what checkpoints to use; he isn't listening.

"I think it's great you're doing it," he says. "I was there ten or fifteen years ago, but not since. My wife's a Jew and can't stand it over there. It reminds her too much of fascism—the Vopos, the streets, the faces."

"And over here—this doesn't remind her?"

"Not so much. But maybe we've been unfair; maybe we should try again. It's important, don't you think? Here we sit, a mile or so away—really a shame, don't you think? So is it true what you tell me? Are there really intelligent people your age over there who stand by their state?"

"Let's say—by their social system. Even if they think of themselves as dissidents, they certainly don't want the Western system."

"But isn't that just because they don't have enough information about the West?"

■ Stevie Wonder is singing on the jukebox as the smoke screen between faces gets thicker and every voice becomes one's own.

"What kind of bar is this? What do they call it now?" asks an old man in a topcoat; he doesn't know if he should sit down. "Egon always used to sit here, that's his chair; yes, and the counter, it's the same one, but all these posters and the young women—what's happened to Egon? Do they even serve beer here anymore?"

■ To the East they build, in the West we renovate, at least on the street where I live. After zigzagging from one house facade to another, the restorers' scaffolding has finally reached my building with its two bar-restaurants. In the dim light of the back courtyard, the boards between their steel supports look like balconies in a theater, and the courtyard looks like the orchestra of an Italian opera house with the roof blown off. The slanting moonbeams spark reflections in the heaps of rubble along the walls and bathe the gallery under the eaves with light. As the courtyard light switches off, the sound of heels announces an entrance.

A woman in a long gown smiles as she comes tripping toward me among the garbage cans; she must have the wrong address. Her blond curls are freshly set and fall against a black stole strewn with little silver stars; gold bracelets chime on her wrists, sparkling jewels hang about her neck. False lashes shimmer on her eyelids, and a fake beauty mark makes the skin over her upper lip look soft and transparent.

"Don't you recognize me?" the lady whispers, and parts her lips in a melting smile. "Haven't you ever heard of Frieda Loch?"

She giggles suggestively, flashes a fishnet-stockinged leg, and swings nimbly around the last garbage can to the door.

"What other Friedas promise, Frieda Loch delivers!" she calls back to me, and coaxes the door key out of her little silver purse.

Only by the sharp, aquiline nose and the voice do I recognize in this fiftyish diva my elderly neighbor, the man behind whose door I had felt lay serenity and a carefree life.

■ Robert first revealed to me the potential seriousness of the phrase "Let's keep in touch." He can almost always be reached by phone, and he expects the same of me. I think I can tell by now, just from the style and vehemence of the ring, whether it's Robert on the line.

Robert's number is busy; it takes twenty minutes to get through. He has been to a car showroom this morning. For weeks now he has been making appointments with dealers over the phone and having them show him what the West has to offer in the way of cars. I don't know how he manages to convince the dealers that he really wants to buy. In his three-day-old beard and

T-shirt, he doesn't exactly look like someone who can pull the cash for a Jaguar out of his back pocket. Yet the fact remains that the dealers always raise the show-room window in order to roll some newly polished jewel onto the street for him.

I guess Robert convinces them less by the extrava-gance than by the impossibility of his demands. Push-button windows, leather seats, and a wooden dashboard are standard equipment for him. But every car that meets these demands leaves something to be desired where body design, leg room, or gearshift is concerned—something that only another make can provide. In any case, Robert can't make up his mind, which is why there's hardly a luxury model around in which he hasn't had himself chauffeured down Kurfürstendamm. Robert finds my ambivalent feelings about these cars narrow-minded. If you're going to live in the Western morass, then by all means do it as comfortably as possible. Rob-ert laughs at class distinctions that West German intel-lectuals draw between a VW Golf, for example, and a Jaguar. He's very orthodox here—he sees them as incon-sistencies within the camp of the bourgeoisie. As long as he has to earn his bread with the enemies of the working class, he prefers to be at the top: after all, Brezhnev would rather deal with the President of the United States than with the chairman of the West Ger-man Communist Party. Since socialism as he understands it can't be implemented here, Robert would just as soon go by the rules of a competitive society—and preferably by those which applied under early capitalism, when they were most explicit. In this he displays the innocence of a conqueror who meets no resistance. With boundless energy he settles himself at the controls of a civilization whose creators have long had one foot in the grave.

This morning Robert has tested an American car that combines almost every impossible feature: leather seats, push-button windows, tinted glass, roomy interior, compact exterior, super speed, and good mileage. He takes me back to the showroom with him; the salesman holds the door open for Robert. As though he'd never even considered any other car, Robert asks the salesman for the technical data on a Mercedes 280 SE.

"Go on, get in," Robert says to me, as the salesman opens the car door for him. "I want to see how it looks on you. Your Citroen is ready for the dump, anyway."

He studies me awhile through the windshield, shakes his head, at first slowly, then more and more emphatically.

"It won't work. You're turning into another person."

Then he shows me the car of his latest dreams.

Before us stands a silver projectile: it has the nose of a jet fighter; over the white leather seats arches a sort of tinted-glass canopy, which allows a panoramic view; the speedometer stops at 150. Robert laughs with me, but I see a combative gleam in his eye.

"Sorry," he says to the salesman, who has begun to hope again. "You can see my friend doesn't like the car."

■ Robert never asks, and won't ask this time, what I've been up to recently. For a long time now, I've been a member of his moderately sized but very close-knit family. I don't need to earn his attention with news; my presence is enough. At the outset I was puzzled by his refusal to show curiosity, let alone surprise. I got the impression that he saw asking questions as a weakness. Later I understood his behavior as a necessary defense, even as a strength which I began to envy. Breaking the commandment "Show no surprise" would expose him to a flood of worries. No matter where he is, Robert stakes out his territory right away and works up a firm routine: newsstand, breakfast café, telephone, post office, bookstore, bar. Give a few people, not too many, your phone number; order the same drink from the same waiter; strike up a conversation with the owner, not the waiter; try out one pinball machine, not three, and get to know that one well. I might have spent the last three months with the Indians along the Amazon—Robert will put a two-mark piece in the machine, let me go first, and then listen once I've lost.

Before we play the next round, I tell him the story of Lutz and the two Willys. Robert listens carefully, thinks for awhile, orders the next round of vodka and beer, and asks without wasting a word on the three moviegoers: "Do you know the story of Walter Bolle, the man who wanted to wage war on the DDR single-handed?"

■ Before his arrival in the West, Walter Bolle had spent a total of seven years in DDR prisons, always for the same offense: illegal border crossing, attempted flight from the DDR, attempted border violation. As a part of the German-German skin trade, he was sold to the West in 1973 for 50,000 West marks. He received his residence permit for the Federal Republic at the emergency reception center in Giessen and left at once for U.S. military headquarters in Heidelberg. Demanding to speak to the head of counterintelligence, he told the sentry that he wanted to plan something against the DDR. He wasn't admitted. He moved into an apartment in a small town in southern Germany, and found a factory job as a metalworker. But since he didn't like piecework or living in a residence with foreign laborers, he quickly gave up his job.

Shortly thereafter Walter Bolle came to the attention of West German police when he stole a Mercedes truck from the factory's parking lot and crashed the border into Austria. He was given a six-month suspended sentence. Then he volunteered for the West German military; he wanted training in sabotage and the use of heavy weapons. The army wanted nothing to do with him. So he offered his services to the French Foreign Legion. They stationed Bolle on Corsica and gave him training in sabotage and heavy weapons, after which he deserted and returned to West Germany via Marseille and Geneva. Once there, he moved in with another deserter whom he had met in the Foreign Legion.

He tried to interest his friend in the following project: each of them would organize a commando group, one in the East and one in the West; then they would advance on a broad front against the Wall and tear it down.

No one, not even his ex-Legionnaire friend, was enthusiastic about Bolle's project. So Bolle went to West

Berlin, jumped the Wall at Lübars, and told the border
guards who seized him that he wanted to come home—
there was nothing happening in the West. After days of
questioning in which the State Security Service took part,
Bolle was informed by an officer of that service that he
would have to prove himself before he came home for
good and all. He would have to go back to the West and
do some work for the State Security Service in order to
show he was worthy of the privilege of living in the
DDR.

At this point the story begins to lose itself in the clouds
of restricted testimony, contradictory statements by
friends, and most of all, Bolle's inconstant memory. Later
he maintained in a West Berlin court that he had an-
ticipated his recruitment, had even sought it out. Of
course he knew that prisoners who have been bought
out of the DDR can't legally return to their country.
That's why he had expected not only his arrest, but also
the attempt to recruit him. He had pretended to go along
because it was the only way to get back to the DDR and
"settle a few accounts." From the beginning he had
planned to infiltrate the State Security Service and be-
tray all his co-workers to the Americans.

It is certain that Bolle carried out missions for the
State Security Service. They piloted him back to the
West along a secret route known as the Ho-Chi-Minh
Trail, and he set right to work. His first job was to follow
his earlier movements in the West and provide the State
Security Service with reports and pictures from each of
his previous stops. No one knows how he felt about this
labor of recollection. But he probably got a certain

satisfaction, if not a sweet sense of revenge, out of photographing the gate to U.S. Headquarters in Heidelberg, skulking through the grounds of his metalworks, photographing the foreman, copying the menu at the workers' canteen, interviewing his onetime companions at the residence, noting their complaints about the misery of piecework and preserving them in invisible ink on sheets of sensitized paper. He must have described the customers at a bar he had once frequented with a similar vengeance, since he was supposed to look out particularly for individuals who were having secret love affairs or who showed homosexual tendencies.

With the information he had gleaned, Bolle returned to the Ho-Chi-Minh Trail at the scheduled time, flashed his identification—the decal of a Leopard tank—at the entrance, and tape-recorded everything he hadn't already written down for his contact officer. His reports proved satisfactory, so he was taken on as a full-time employee of the Ministry for State Security and sent back to the West with new instructions. As ordered, he presented himself to the West Berlin political police and revealed that he was a DDR agent. He told his interrogator the incredible story of his progress—how the leader of a projected war against the DDR had become a collaborator in the Ministry for State Security—with one slight twist that may actually have been the truth: he claimed to have signed on with the Stasi only in order to qualify for the work he really wanted with Western intelligence. Then he willingly described his Eastern contact officer, gave away the man's cover, described a gold cap in his right lower jaw and a wristwatch he wore too high, probably to hide a tattoo. The only facts Bolle suppressed were that he was leaking all this on orders from the East, and that he was memorizing the corresponding features of his Western interrogator.

It is probable, though not certain, that the West Berlin political police also recruited Bolle as an agent. The fact that he wasn't arrested speaks for itself. Whether he was on a single or a double mission, it is known for sure that Bolle returned to the Ho-Chi-Minh Trail soon after unmasking himself, in order to report on his visit to the other side. In the process he was able to use almost all the phrases he had put down in the West Berlin protocol describing his Eastern chief and the man's office. Aside from the names of the heads of state whose framed portraits hung on the wall behind each of the enemy chiefs, and aside from the difference between a gold and an amalgam filling, a Zeiss and a Swiss watch, the texts proved identical. A quote from Stalin that Bolle had learned in school applied neatly: "Leaders come and go, but the German people remain." For the word "people," he substituted "lampshade," "wallpaper," "office chair."

From this point in the story, it is impossible to make out for whom or what Bolle was working: the East, the West, himself, or a united Germany—even Bolle probably no longer knew.

He subsequently joined an ad hoc committee of free Berliners and took part in propaganda campaigns, particularly those directed against the Wall. Soon he attracted attention in the group by trying to radicalize its activities. He proposed that they attack the S-Bahn, form an armed defensive unit, drop leaflets from balloons sent over the Wall. His fierceness made the group leader suspicious. The leader felt that Bolle was taking an overly literal approach to the committee's declaration of war on the abuses of the socialist system, and he did his best to keep Bolle out of the real action. Bolle got his revenge by telling his Eastern contact officer that the leader was a homosexual. He also gave him credit for a project that existed only in Bolle's mind: setting up an illegal radio transmitter for propaganda that would prepare all Germans to march against the Wall. To his Western contact officer, Bolle described the same project as a provocation engineered by the East.

Still, he won the serious attention of both secret services only when he set up the ominous transmitter himself. From a garret in Kreuzberg he preached war against the Wall—and so for awhile managed to carry out a part of his original plan. He confirmed the cartoon-like perception each state had of its opposite number, and by playing their projections off against each other, he lived out his own madness. Paradoxically, he could take every step in his double-crossing game with conviction. Participating in the operations of the free Berliners' committee must have seemed as right to him as revealing those operations to the State Security Service. Betraying his Eastern contact officer to his Western counterpart must have seemed as necessary as the reverse. Walter Bolle had got himself into a situation where he stayed truest to himself when he betrayed each German state to the other on orders from both.

Bolle went astray only when he noticed that neither

of his employers was interested in destroying the transmitter. Both were awaiting developments, presumably for greater media effect when each did finally accuse the other of political meddling. At this juncture, Bolle recalled the starting point of his enterprise and set off again for U.S. counterintelligence. There he presented himself as an American collaborator who had been working without pay for a year. Under questioning, it became clear that Bolle hadn't met an operative other than his contact officer in his whole time at the State Security Service. All he could supply was the officer's code name, his physical features, and a few details of his office decor.

The Americans treated Bolle as an East German spy and turned him over to the West Berlin courts. In his summation, by contrast, the High Court judge characterized the defendant as a lost man, someone who, in his confusion, had declared a single-handed war on the DDR. The sentence, furthermore, was based on the fact that Bolle had only endangered people in the West. He was given a ten-month suspended term, including his pre-trial incarceration. When I asked for Walter Bolle's address at the central housing office, they told me that he had left for parts unknown, but that a lot of people had asked after him.

■ Robert and I sit outside in the balmy evening; the tables and chairs of our bar are filled with customers. As the lights go on along Kurfürstendamm, a young man steps up to our table. A kerchief hanging around his neck is knotted so it can easily be pulled up as a mask. His overalls and work shirt mark him as part of the generation that seems intent on wearing out their fathers' work clothes.

"You'd better move on," he tells us, in the voice of an unusually polite cop. "Some people will be along shortly to smash in the windows."

"What's happened?"

"Someone starved to death in the maximum security wing."

Customers jump up from their tables, crowd around the waitress to settle accounts before the heralded slaughter begins. Those who have just paid hurry to their cars and speed off, motors roaring. Iron grilles rattle down, left and right; but you can already hear the smash, the clattering rain of heavy glass, and then the burglar alarms in the stores, howling like mortally wounded animals.

"I'm staying put," I say to Robert. "They'll break up the jeweler's on the right and the car showroom on the left, but not Charlie's windows. They'll be coming in for a beer after they've done their work."

Robert has stood up, his urge to flight conflicting with his desire to join in. There are barely thirty of them, young people casually strolling down Kurfürstendamm. Their faces are masked by particolored kerchiefs, their bodies are as thin as a hunger striker's, the women recognizable only by their softer movements and narrower shoulders under the oversized shirts. Several are carrying sacks made out of kerchiefs; they take out stones and pass them to other demonstrators, who run and throw them.

In the past ten years it has gotten harder to destroy a showroom window. I watch a boy about seventeen with the wrists of a girl; his stone hits the window over and over, bouncing to the sidewalk like a rubber ball. Only when he takes a running start before he throws does the glass respond with a short, undramatic plop. The hole, no bigger than the stone, immediately develops crystallized edges, radiates thin cracks across the glass surface. At the same time, apparently all by itself, the glass emits a long scream which blends with the sirens of the other security systems. A choir lifts its many voices, each one a bat's frequency away from the others; it's as if the display windows were following the score of a twelve-tone composition, which they perform only when hit.

The procession, as it conducts this choir with identical repetitive throwing motions, is almost horde-like in its muteness. It moves leisurely down Kurfürstendamm along the newly polished brass-trimmed storefronts, newly washed display windows, renovated facades, scoured and hosed sidewalks. As it goes it pits the dialogue of stones and burglar alarms against the sound of motors and the rumbling of the U-Bahn, which has been muffled to the level of drawing-room conversation. The spectacle reminds me of a scene from an Italian wide-screen production: this is what it must have been like when the Germanic tribes, armed only with axes and clubs, overwhelmed the colossal, decaying Roman empire.

"They're so cool about it! It's unbelievable!" says Robert, with an atavistic gleam in his eyes. "It's the collapse of state power."

"What do you mean, collapse? The police have been taken by surprise, that's all."

"You don't believe that yourself. In the DDR, the cops would be here in three minutes flat. All the side streets blocked off, the U-Bahn entrances occupied, everyone rounded up in five minutes and off to the factory."

The gang has moved on; the smashing of glass and the scream of alarms fades like a storm on the horizon. We sit by ourselves in the street, now almost empty. We can make out gentlemen in suits behind the display windows, holding either a telephone or a broom and venting their anger on the broken glass, which they vehemently heave out into the street. Then they stand silent guard over their goods, which are now suddenly accessible.

"It was only a rumor; no one starved," says the waiter. He has just been listening to the news.

"They figured that one out nicely," says Robert.

"What?"

"Oh, come on! First someone stops by and politely asks us to take cover. Then, at a calculated distance, the stoning gang comes along and peacefully smashes in the windows from the Gedächtniskirche to Halensee. We've been sitting here for an hour now, and there isn't a police van in sight, not even a patrol! You can't fool me! This was a set-up!"

"You think those kids we saw were really plainclothes police?"

"Not all of them; just the leaders."

"And what would the police have been after?"

Robert looks at me as if I were a child, blind to the last piece of a puzzle that is staring him in the face.

"You heard it yourself: nobody died. The whole operation was based on a rumor and that's how the public will see it. But someone will die soon enough. Then there won't be any protest, because the demonstrators were wrong the first time. And the police will have an excuse for cordoning off the inner city before any real demonstration occurs."

Robert's proofs usually have a certain appeal; you're forced to think them over before dismissing them.

"And you want me to believe that the police worked it all out in advance? That they first spread a rumor, then staged a false protest so they can prevent a real one when the rumor comes true?"

"What else!"

"That's crazy! That was a spontaneous demonstration. And the police didn't come in time precisely because it was spontaneous."

"Your notion of the state is touchingly naïve. You look at it with your child's eyes and believe what you see."

"And you think the state is omnipotent. Everything that happens is preprogrammed, monitored, controlled by invisible hands. You didn't live through the student movement."

"Lay off with your student movement! It was manipulated from above, just like everything else. Who brought the first bombs into that movement?"

"You don't know a thing about it."

"Want to bet? You'll find it in Hegel: the Quislings of history—"

"You're misquoting. The expression 'Quislings' doesn't appear in Hegel. Quote Marx if you want, but leave Hegel out of it; you haven't even read him!"

"That does it! I haven't read Hegel? You and your Western arrogance! What do you know . . ."

"I said the expression doesn't occur in Hegel!"

"Want to bet? A case of champagne!"

"Fine. Just to make you stop running on about things you don't know."

"And you—you're just conforming. You've gone diaper-soft, a nice Social Democrat. The state has you on a long leash, so you think you've got freedom to move."

"Maybe you can write poems with your paranoia, but stay out of politics!"

"Say that again and I'll knock your teeth in!"

"I said, with your paranoia—"

"Waiter, the check. I can't stand you Western creeps, you Social Democrats. I've wasted too much time on you . . . you're so . . . just the way you live—how do you live? You looked on with the same naïvete while the Nazis—"

"You better shut your mouth, or I'm going to shut it for you!"

We've been on our feet for some time now, yelling at each other amid the broken glass. As a pale light rises over the rooftops, I see us striking out at each other with weary, weighted blows, angrily babbling our lessons, true to the states whose influence we no longer recognize.

■ It isn't our first fight of this kind. We listen to a news broadcast together, look at a picture in the paper, witness an incident and get two different messages out of the same thing. The quarrel begins when I take what I see at face value; Robert has been trained to read between the lines. Where I perceive merely an event, maybe an accident, Robert perceives a plan he has to decipher. A friend who in my view is shy, in Robert's view is only pretending to be shy. A colleague doesn't just succeed; he has a formula for success. As Robert sees it, Western society is essentially a well-organized syndicate deliberately kept in a state of disorder by a few people in the know. Whether consciously or not, every impulse within the society follows a plan for the benefit of the bosses: coincidences, accidents are built in; the world is controlled by the secret services. Spontaneity, personal initiative, free choice—these ideals of Western society are fairy tales invented for people who don't want to admit they know better.

The advantage of his delusion is that the blame always falls on something outside him. For good or for bad, Robert is sheltered by a state that takes responsibility for everything; Robert himself is never to blame.

As I consider this objection, it turns itself around. Who derives benefits from which way of thinking? Doesn't every career in Western society, whether that of an athlete, investor, artist, or rebel, depend upon the assumption that every initiative is one's own, every idea original, every decision completely personal? What would happen to me if I stopped finding fault with myself, as I've been taught to do, and blamed everything on the state? Where does a state end and a self begin?

In any case, my delusion—if it is one—is more likely than Robert's to bring success on this side of the Wall.

■ A white sun is rising at the end of Kurfürstendamm; empty of people, the street looks scoured; it is so still you can hear the traffic lights clicking as they change. As we walk side by side down the gently sloping street, I suddenly wish we could keep on moving. A forgotten notion resurfaces, one which I associated with Robert when I first met him: someday we would go on a trip together with no other purpose than to keep going; we would part in one city and meet again in another, follow a path until our point of departure had turned into the vanishing point. Why have we stayed on here in the shadow of walls, where every word, every thought resounds like the echo of something uttered long ago and in vain?

At his corner, Robert stops. "We're so—" he begins, then breaks off, as though to avoid driving away a clear feeling with too precise an expression.

"We're much too cautious with each other—and much too careless," he says then. "Forget just once what you know about me; don't label me so quickly! I bet if you saw a horn growing out of my forehead right now, you'd instantly come up with the reason."

The cacophony of waking birds echoes from the rear courtyards as we say goodbye. Toward noon Robert will call up, ask how I've slept, and bring last night's quarrel into the light of day. Later he'll put on one of his favorite records and turn the volume way up; he knows that we hear the same message in those heavy, reclusive songs accompanied by an organ, a saxophone, and violins.

What did we fight about? Was it really Robert I was fighting with? Once before I had to go through this struggle between two ways of seeing; once before I had to cope with the feeling that someone was trying to take control of my mental processes.

■ The image I first formed of Lena grew out of an indefinable yearning for completion, for an experience which lay outside of me and couldn't be brought within bounds. What attracted me to her wasn't so much the mystery in her looks, as the sense that I might never figure it out: a rigor and a vulnerability in her face that at the same time belied those words; a laughter you couldn't share. To say this yearning was linked to a geographic direction would be pure hindsight. But a scenario not of our creation took over when, after Brassens songs and flamenco tunes, I played a few bars of a Russian gypsy romance for her on the guitar. I could only imitate the text phonetically, and she corrected me: *Vsya dusha polna tashkayu.*

I had learned these songs from records, but Lena had heard them evening after evening through the windows of a Russian barracks across the street from her apartment in a small Mecklenburg town. Her stories of life on the other side of the Wall seemed like fairy tales to me:

the *komsomoltsy* Lena watched from her window as they jumped bare-chested over obstacles during their morning exercises; the voices, the bits of conversation, the songs which drifted over to her in the evening from the barracks and mingled with the stories she remembered from Dostoevsky and Chekhov; her brief love for a Russian pilot who seduced her in the cockpit of his fighter plane, flew into the sky with her, and on landing disappeared forever. Images of skating on frozen lakes, of white-trunked birches in the springtime, of harvesting crews in the summer—these gave an impression of a faraway, an unattainable world.

Some of these stories, particularly those which took place after Lena moved to Berlin, did turn out to be fairy tales. Of course, the Italian count who offered Lena his hand and his castles couldn't be reminded of his promise—he had died in a car accident. But another lover, who was supposedly traveling through Mexico on horseback in a vain attempt to forget her, turned out after a while to be the repulsive book dealer lurking around my apartment door in the evenings, a habit he retained well after Lena and I were no longer coming home together. If she had been from Munich, I imagine I would have recommended that she get treatment for her mythomania. But Lena's stories seemed to me the product of a wishing so strong that the conditional past became the past pure and simple; they were not lies.

She had an overwhelming need for acceptance, which expressed itself more in gestures than in words: sometimes when she was standing or walking beside me, she would suddenly let herself fall, as though testing to see whether I would catch her. Or she would take a few steps back after we had embraced, and run toward me again as if to make sure that I was the one taking her in his arms. When we parted, her posture expressed a similar distrust: she would stand there defiantly for a moment, again as though about to fall. Any distance that went beyond arm's length seemed too far.

Her need for uninterrupted closeness was only increased by her sense of constant rejection by life in the West. Like a black on Manhattan's Fifth Avenue, Lena recoiled at everything as she moved along the shopping streets of West Berlin. For her the West was a tangle of contradictions, half-hearted gestures, and empty promises; another continent, eternal ice beneath a superficial warmth. Acquaintances were made only to be broken off; names exchanged to be forgotten the next day; calls promised, although you knew they would never come. False smiles, false teeth. Her political disillusion focused not so much on the anti-Communism of the society as on the cocktail-party tone of that anti-Communism—a tone which took nothing seriously. The politicians were alcoholics, with the puffy lids of all-night drunks; they meant nothing they said. The West was false and deceitful, and Lena, with a child's sense of truth, insisted on the literal meaning of words.

Her refusal to feel at home over here emphasized my own discomfort. Lena's experience was superior to mine, and that gave her a kind of authority. Her defiant, aggressive stance filled me with pride, as though I were braving a danger that my friends avoided. Only later did I notice Lena's habit of nodding in recognition when

I told her something she couldn't possibly know. It was as if a question, a mark of surprise would rob her of something she would never regain. Sometimes I used foreign words on purpose, to make her ask me for the meaning. "Why are you nodding, Lena, there's no way you can know that; you aren't exposing yourself by asking a question." But she classified all my experiences or observations with an instant gesture of agreement or rejection, and took them as symptoms of an attitude. Lena read whole biographies in the lines of a face, turns of phrase, postures. She felt that acquaintances were adequately described by their inability to look her in the eyes when they spoke. A statement like, "I'll take the check; I can write it off," was enough to make her send me a meaningful glance, and I was supposed to share in the secret. A picture in the paper or a synopsis was all she needed to evaluate a film: "We can skip that one." Beneath Lena's glance, people invariably gave themselves away. Her whole perceptive apparatus seemed increasingly geared toward finding someone out; and since she was looking for the flaw, she always found it. Invariably the person—through the car he drove, the apartment he lived in, the bar he patronized—revealed his share in the system of repression and exploitation.

After a period of trust founded on the senses of touch and smell, the distrust that had settled in the corners of Lena's mouth directed itself at me. Hers was a suspicion that interpreted my every independent step into the world as an attempted escape. I went on a trip alone to a distant country only at the price of mortally wounding her; faced with her pain, any reason to travel lost

validity. A call from an ex-girlfriend, a solitary evening
at the bar, a stain on the bed sheet revealed contacts
with a world we had sworn to resist. Lena's need for my
company expressed itself first as suspicion of everything
that took me away from her, then as suspicion of me:
"The bar isn't open this late, why do you even go there,
the other day you said your friends were getting on your
nerves." It could take hours to reconstruct the process
by which a ballpoint pen that didn't belong to me had
found its way into my pocket. A fight started with her
questioning whether I had bought an issue of *Konkret*
because of an article by Rudi Dutschke or a bared breast.
It went on for days. My claim that I had bought it solely
because of Dutschke made everything worse; besides,
it wasn't true.

I responded to Lena's suspicion first by protesting
violently against it, then by giving it cause. Only with
her hanging over me did I venture to satisfy needs I had
long postponed: I traveled, renewed friendships that had
previously seemed superficial, developed a sudden taste
for stag parties. The more often I left Lena, the more
desperately she tried to coerce my presence. More and
more, I would stand by impassively while she got herself into dangerous situations.

In the line at a ticket window in Copenhagen, she
suddenly leaned on me from behind. A man I had noticed earlier because of his deeply pockmarked face had
grabbed her hair and pulled her head back. When I
turned around, he was gone. Her fingers would dig into
my arm at the sight of another persecutor who always
dressed in black, crossed our path often in Berlin, and

would suddenly reappear behind us when we thought we had lost him. She felt a destructive force emanating from him, something murderous; she said that one day he would find her alone and kill her, shoot her from behind. Then there were the slow-moving Mercedes, the lowered windows behind which nameless faces asked her price, the lurking shadows in entryways, the glances at rush hour that bored into her breasts, the obscene whispers, the groping hands.

Lena was exposed to all these attacks because I had left her alone; any attempt to play them down betrayed me as an accomplice. In the course of a few months she had identified me as a shareholder in a corrupt system. Our coordinates were now fixed: I was the spoiled one, easily seduced, incapable of forming relationships. She had always had a harder time of it and as a result knew what she wanted: she was decisive, pure, quick to judge. Our struggle raged into the realm of grammar itself. Allusions, metaphors, ambiguities in my sentences were an attempt to hide something; the use of the subjunctive, even when grammatically appropriate, was artificial, showed lack of feeling and directness. Lena loathed irony above all: it was a way of speaking that skirted the question of exact meaning. You should behave forthrightly, speak plainly, take a stand; the despicable opposite of that was to change your opinions overnight, talk one way and act another, avoid saying what you think.

To catch Lena in her own contradictions was like threatening her existence. To her there was no need to repeat an experience you had already been through: her response was, I've had that experience. A sentence once uttered was a contract for eternity: I've said that from the beginning, and I stand by it. Any departure from the main clause, from the indicative, awoke the suspicion of something superfluous: You may need that, but I don't. Her disgust at the superfluous extended to the body. The trace of a paunch, the beginnings of a double chin, were signs of an ambiguous life-style; they triggered a hunt for causes. "Frank people, straight people are a worthy aim," goes a song by a woman protest singer in the DDR. This longing for frankness and resolution revealed the effect, even on dissidents, of a state education in steadfast loyalty, militant commitment, and iron determination.

At first we quarreled over how to evaluate our perceptions, then over the perceptions themselves. Had a friend said the insulting words the way Lena quoted them? Had I or had I not promised to be home before midnight? Had I or had I not said I never wanted to see so-and-so again? Were those sounds from next door cries of pleasure or of pain? Lena's injured gaze always focused on details which escaped me. What I missed rebounded as guilt: the gap in my perception revealed complicity with the hostile world of men out there, and I began to confess. Most of all, I couldn't deal with the pain I caused her by questioning her judgment and standing by my own—I couldn't compete with her chest pains and fevers by debating about our perceptions.

So I gradually acquired Lena's point of view, learned it like a foreign language without comprehending its inner structure. I began to hear friends' comments through Lena's ears, to suffer beneath men's eyes as though I were their quarry, to shrink from bare breasts at the newsstand as though they ridiculed my sex, to use Lena's words in describing the city where I too was a stranger, though in a different way. It reached the point where, head down and without saying hello, I would steal by friends with whom I had spent years of my life. I had entered the enclosure that Lena had erected around herself; the world beyond the fence was something extraneous, of which I had to purge myself.

■ Something is wrong with Pommerer's phone. Even when I wait between each of the ten numbers, I can't get a ring at the other end. On another try I go six digits, then tune into a conversation between two women.

"And how's Ulli?"

"He came back exhausted from volleyball. Dizzy spells."

"Is he in bed again?"

"Oh yes, with a hot-water bottle."

"Men are so ridiculously ambitious—and good for nothing afterwards. Say, are you alone in the room? What's the story with Stefan? Just say yes or no. Are you moving in together or not?"

"No."

"So it isn't the real thing?"

"Oh yes, it is."

I lose the connection and dial Pommerer's number again.

"And you haven't said anything to Ulli about it yet?"

"No."

"It must be a tough decision."

"Yes."

"But you're still seeing Stefan?"

"Yes."

"But you don't want to risk everything on that."

"No."

"Well, the main thing is for Ulli to get back on his feet. Is he listening in? I hear a kind of panting . . ."

A pause follows. I hang up and try again, only to get the same voices.

"So what do you think about Andreas?"

"At first I didn't think anything. I just started bawling."

"I only cried later, at church. I was just so shocked. It was all so unexpected."

"I wouldn't say that."

"You mean you expected the accident?"

"Well, I wasn't surprised."

Finally I managed to dial all ten numbers. This time the static from the receiver sounds like the DDR phone system. But instead of a ring, I hear a fine, even *bing-bing*, like a needle falling on a metal plate.

4

■ The best time to cross the border at Heinrich Heine Strasse is between twelve and two in the afternoon. The checkpoint is almost empty: just one other traveler, with a shepherd dog on a leash, waits under the loudspeaker for his number to be called. I could simply drive up to the shed from which a border official will soon emerge to hand me my numbered ticket. But I know the consequences of crossing the white line unasked: the officer, even if he is there and ready, will wave me back and make me wait until he gives me a sign. I can't follow impulse: I have to wait for his beckoning hand, and I can't afford to miss it. The message in this ritual is clear and seems deliberate: I am entering a state where even things that will happen anyway require authorization.

Once I've collected my number and parked the Citroen in response to a second wave, I pay the road user's fee, exchange the minimum amount of West marks, and station myself beside the man with the shepherd. The seat behind the booth through which they return the passports is empty. It will take ten to fifteen minutes before they call me. Even without the traffic, that's the minimum wait—like the decompression halt a diver has to make coming up from the depths.

A meditative silence ensues. At the checkpoint the road slaloms between three-foot-high concrete walls decorated with petunias, runs into a one-lane track lined by border officials' sheds, and then widens to a street sloping up gently beyond the barrier, where it loses itself on a false horizon. The facades along the street are like memories of houses, and the border strip gives the impression of a parched riverbed that has narrowed permanently between the sheds—at this point, any flow would come too late.

The officer has disappeared into his shed. The man waiting beside me stares vacantly at the twitching coat of his dog, as though it concealed the last motion possible here. From time to time he whispers brief commands, as if to check his voice and the dog's readiness to respond. I notice that a face has filled the booth window only when a throat is cleared over the loudspeaker. Maybe the officer has left the door to his cell open, because there is a strong draft through the slit in the window. He smacks his hand down on the dog owner's papers as if he were killing a fly.

The dog's ears tremble at the slamming hand and the rustling papers. When its master's number is called over the loudspeaker, the dog goes up on its hind legs; its face appears at the window, as though for identification. The dog begins barking, and the officer has a hard time controlling his jolt of fright. The stiff collar of his uniform digs a white furrow into his neck; the furrow quickly fills with blood as the officer leans forward and barks back at the dog through the microphone. The tenfold amplification drives the dog to wilder barking. The officer barks back lustily; both their noses are almost bumping the glass, which clouds up with man and dog breath. Neither wants to yield; the officer stretches his neck far out of the uniform, slaps his thighs with pleasure, and barks until the whole checkpoint echoes with the sound.

It seems an eternity before the dog's owner pulls it back by the collar and the officer's barking turns into peals of laughter. Still gasping for breath, he slides the owner's papers through the slit. The ear check won't be necessary; one dog lover has found another. His good mood affects the other border officials. The customs man leafs amicably through a book I hand him.

"Well, if you wrote this yourself, I guess you can tell me what's in it."

I recall a short review of my stories. "They're just tales about love that doesn't work out."

"That's fine. You can take 'em in."

■ Pommerer can't give a yes or a no to the question of whether his phone is out of order. For a couple of days it has worked only in one direction: he can make calls, but doesn't receive any.

Pommerer and some of his colleagues wrote to the chairman of the State Council several weeks ago. They requested that he reverse the decision to levy a large fine on a writer who had published a novel in the West without permission from the DDR copyright office. Since then the rumor is that the authors of the letter face exclusion from the writers' union.

The faulty connection between Pommerer's phone and the outside world may stem from the letter. But it could also be simply a technical problem.

"Since Lenin's dream came true and the state started operating on the model of the German post office," Pommerer says, "communications haven't done so well."

Later he says: "All we have here is a double-barreled shotgun and two cartridges. We fired the first when we protested against Wolf Biermann's exile. This letter was the second. Now we've used up our ammunition; the only question is, did we pick the right time for the second shot?"

"Didn't you think it over carefully?"

"I don't know. I felt really good right after we sent it off. But it was the feeling you get from spontaneous action—and it may have put an end to spontaneity for years to come."

■ At Pommerer's favorite bar the waiter greets us as usual. The room is almost empty; the loudest sound comes from the ventilator. I last heard Stevie Wonder's voice at Charlie's, with Robert—now here it is again.

"How's your work going?" Pommerer asks.

"Every story lacks something that the next one has; but then the next story is missing something from the one before. Maybe the story I'm looking for doesn't exist."

I tell Pommerer the one about Walter Bolle, who wanted to wage war on the DDR single-handed. Pommerer listens carefully, thinks awhile, orders the next round of vodka and beer, and then asks without wasting a word on Bolle: "Do you know the story of Michael Gartenschläger and his twenty-two thousand comrades?"

■ Michael Gartenschläger from Berlin-Straussberg was seventeen when the Wall went up. A few hours after its construction, he and four friends painted anti-Ulbricht slogans and nationalistic graffiti on the new surface. He was arrested five days later—after he had burned down the barn of an agricultural cooperative. Following a three-day show trial, the court sentenced him to life for sabotage compounded by violence and propaganda threatening the security of the state. DDR newspapers made much of Gartenschläger as a "locksmith who listened to American Sector radio broadcasts," "an arsonist and vandal," "an outlaw who should be banned from society." At Brandenburg Penitentiary, where he completed grade ten of the Polytechnic and earned his lathe operator's certificate, he did his best to live up to his reputation. During a seventeen-month stretch in solitary confinement, he climbed the 183-foot chimney of the penitentiary and demanded more bread for prisoners in solitary: he wanted not ten but twenty ounces a day. On another occasion he was put in chains because he passed money to another prisoner for an escape attempt. Two of his own tries at escaping failed. Only after ten years was Gartenschläger ransomed by the government of the other German state for 45,000 West marks.

Gartenschläger settled in Hamburg, where he leased a gas station. From the beginning he considered his freedom only an opportunity to vent the hatred he had stored up during ten years in confinement. To set someone or something free from the DDR—that had become his goal in life.

Gartenschläger spent his first years in the West helping would-be emigrants to escape. He organized escapes via Yugoslavia and passport switches in Libya. For months he worked on a plan to kidnap the DDR's minister of defense and bring him into the Federal Republic. He gave the project up when he began to feel he was being shadowed on his visits to most East bloc countries. In the idle weeks that followed, he toyed with the idea of liberating diamonds from a cache in South Africa. Then he came across the newspaper story that gave his obsession its definitive form.

The story reported that 22,000 self-triggering robots had been installed along the East German border with the Federal Republic since 1971. Western experts knew only what the robots did, not how they worked. At the slightest vibration of the border fence, a detonator would set off a propellant charge which would fire a hundred or so sharp-edged metal cubes in a fan-shaped trajectory. The mechanisms were so sensitive that a "perch wire" had to be rigged a couple of inches above the trip wire to prevent blackbirds, thrushes, finches, and starlings from setting it off. Since several of the devices were mounted side by side at each border fence post, the metal cubes could spray over everything within a radius of 80 feet. They had an effect like that of dum-dum bullets.

The story said that the mechanism had never been seen in the West, and Gartenschläger heard this as a summons. One March night he blacked his face and hands with soot and, together with an assistant, crept up to a fence post on the border that he had carefully selected beforehand. The post, which was near Büchen in Lower Saxony, stood on broken terrain covered with bushes and pines. Gartenschläger sowed a quarter-pound of pepper around the post to ward off the DDR police dogs; his assistant, bound to him by 165 feet of fishing line, watched for Western border patrols.

At about two in the morning, Gartenschläger climbed his ladder and set to work dismantling the robot he had selected. Later he always referred to it as "my comrade." His comrade confronted him with a life-and-death choice of the one cable among several that would interrupt detonator contact rather than trigger the charge. Through technical intuition compounded with reckless courage, he found the right cable and took the mechanism apart. Then Gartenschläger and his assistant set to work and raised a commotion, because they were determined to photograph the bewildered look on the face of the DDR border guard who discovered the damage. Nothing at all happened.

Gartenschläger celebrated his triumph for several weeks. He sold his comrade for 12,000 West marks to a West German newsmagazine, which had it examined by scientists and published the results. Gartenschläger found a large audience for his malicious pleasure, since he was written up by the whole West German press. Public excitement reached its peak when a West Berlin journalist reported in the same newsmagazine that the robots had been invented by an SS group leader named Lutter for concentration camp fences. In 1945 the Soviets made off with the blueprints, as yet incomplete, and later offered them to the DDR's secret service. During the fifties they were turned over for further development to a group of eight specially selected prisoners at Hohenschönhausen's so-called Intelligence Detention Facility. By 1960 blueprints for the machines were ready, but they went into line production only in 1969, at Schönebeck Munitions Plant on the Elbe.

Meanwhile Gartenschläger found himself drawn back to the border, to his 21,999 other comrades. Less than four weeks later he dismantled another robot about 40 miles south of Büchen. But this one was seized at his apartment, and the district attorney in Lübeck charged him with "theft of third-party property." Gartenschläger didn't let that prevent him from reconnaissance along the border. Once, from a distance of six feet, he yelled to the DDR border guards: "Don't look so tough! I'll take you for a third and a fourth one!"

His plans had grown more ambitious: he wanted to take a third comrade together with a piece of metal fencing and attach it to the flagpole of the DDR Mission in Bonn. One May Day Gartenschläger returned to the border forest near Büchen. Actually, he was just going with two companions to collect the ladder he had left in the bushes after his first successful mission. Once he came to the spot where the ladder was hidden, however, the metal fence must have exerted an irresistible attraction. His two assistants were already walking off with the ladder under their arms when Gartenschläger turned back to the fence. "Fuck it, I'll just pick off another comrade before we leave; I won't be a second."

Gartenschläger must have known, or at least suspected, that special surveillance had been laid on at the fence after his first coup—that searchlights had been installed and an observation bunker built. There is also some question about how hard Gartenschläger's companions really tried to keep him from returning to the fence. One of them later turned himself in to the Federal Republic's security authorities as an employee of DDR State Security. Gartenschläger went back alone to the site where he had dismantled his first comrade. But as he stretched his hand out for the comrade that had replaced it, he was riddled by fire from several Kalashnikov automatic rifles.

■ Pommerer has been speaking in a low voice; now he falls silent and the rasp of the ventilator sounds out again.

"Pommerer?" a voice asks suddenly, so close to us that Pommerer starts before nodding. A young man has stepped up to our table; he looks at us as if we were old friends, says "Waiter, a round for the gentlemen and myself—may I?" and, without pausing for an answer, pulls a chair up to the table with his high-heeled boot. Pommerer seems to be searching his memory for some previous meeting with this stranger, who grins at us like one who is always sure of his welcome. He is wearing a black leather jacket; the mother-of-pearl buttons on his denim shirt are unbuttoned, revealing his curly-haired chest; a gold chain hangs around his neck.

"Keep it up—don't give in!" he says, and waves a fist with thumb erect in front of Pommerer's face. "When the going gets rough, you can join our plant. We'll see you through!"

Pommerer stares at him helplessly.

"I heard about your letter on TV. Great! Just don't skip town!"

"But why would I want to join your plant? What do you do there?" Pommerer asks.

"Specialist in the movement of goods," the stranger replies. "I prefer to say shipping clerk. They've just demoted me some, because I'm kind of a troublemaker, too. But what can happen to me? At worst they send you into the factories, and I'm already there. What I wanted to tell you: if we both, you and I . . . you know, together we could . . ."

"What?" Pommerer asks.

"If we all pull together, we'll come out on top," the shipping clerk recites, and laughs.

"Listen," Pommerer says cautiously, "this is just a private conversation."

"I noticed," the shipping clerk says, and downs his vodka. He thinks for a while, orders another vodka, and then asks, without wasting a word on Gartenschläger: "Do you know the story of Butterfly, our ambassador to China? Butterfly is a bit odd, but so is everyone at the plant. Take me, making faces at the foreman behind his back—I get that mad. Butterfly used to greet him every day with: 'Good morning, my golden sun!' Butterfly grew up in an orphanage, he doesn't have any teeth, he's bald, he can't find a woman, but he works enough for three. So Butterfly pockets a couple of television tubes at the plant and gets caught. They search his apartment and find West marks. Now, where did he get West marks? He fished them out of the fountain at Alexanderplatz. Tourists from all the German provinces dump marks in there. The only difference is, the West marks are made of nickel, the East marks are aluminum. Can Butterfly help it if only West marks stick to his fishing magnet? Some nights he pulled as much as ten marks out of the fountain. And I wonder: is he just dumb, or has he lost his marbles? He's a smart bastard!

"But of course no one believes his fish story; they take him to the plant doctor. So there's Butterfly, standing in front of the doctor, who has already checked his mental condition on several occasions. The doctor asks the classic questions: Is he depressed, would he rather live somewhere else, be someone else? Sure, says Butterfly, how about ambassador? Where? Well, as far away as possible; in China. So you want to be ambassador to China, says the plant doctor—who, by the way, is a woman, and what a woman! Butterfly has had his eye on her for some time, and since his answer seems to please her, he repeats it coolly: Sure, what else! Ambassador to China! So they committed him to a mental hospital. We called him Butterfly, because he was always humming that song to himself: 'Butterfly, you fly so high, we'll meet in China by and by.'

"When I heard what had happened to Butterfly, I flipped out. I went to the foreman and said: 'The sun rises in the East and sets in the West! Wang doi feng! Peng Peng!' This went on for a while, until they asked for my identity card. They then discovered that I'd pasted slogans all over the plastic card case: Rolling Stones, Fuck it, Let's go West, Coca Cola, and all that shit. So there was trouble. Nonstop cops, questions about the slogans, until I thought—I'll fix them. I put a handwritten note in with my ID that said: 'This is my socialist fatherland; I'm happy here. I love the DDR. Long Live the German Socialist Unity Party! DDR—USSR: Friends Forever!' From then on, they left me in peace! I swear it! What could they do? They're not allowed to doubt. They're so gullible! If they weren't constantly trying to beat into us how good we have it, we might be willing to admit that things aren't so bad. But they lie so much, you can't even believe them when they tell the truth. What was I saying?"

"Another double!" Pommerer answers.

"Right, but would you give me your telephone number—I mean, the two of us, if we could both, that is, together we could really . . ."

"My phone is out of order," says Pommerer, relieved.

On the way home, he says: "If you could travel out, come back, and leave again, this would be the best place in the world."

"Why?"

"Because of the people. They're more serious, more committed, hungrier."

A remark it would be difficult to prove, like all comments that generalize a feeling, an observation. Yet it seems right to me, though at the same time I have another impression that pushes for generalization: Pommerer, an intellectual under socialism, has about as much contact with the workers as I do in the West. He gets to know them when a water main bursts, a facade is restored, or a chair stands vacant at a barroom table.

■ The next day we're sitting in front of the evening news. The strikes in Poland: the Eastern anchor man reports what *Pravda* and the Polish Party organ, *Tribuna Ludu*, have to say. Anti-socialist elements incited by the West European powers are sowing chaos and anarchy. On the same subject, the Western anchor man quotes exclusively from statements by the Polish Solidarity Union. He adds that the Party organ's campaign against anti-socialist elements is picking up. Network executives on both sides are laughably alike: in their own camp, they let only the rulers speak; in the enemy camp, only the oppressed.

Afterwards we watch a program on West German TV about the history of the German partition. They have added color to the documentary footage of bombed-out Berlin, as if only the fullest technical exploitation of the medium could bring out the horror. It becomes obvious that there is no life behind the house fronts left standing when a woman's form appears at the edge of the screen, searching through the ruins.

"At the time," the commentator says, "experts calculated that it would take ten freight trains a day for sixteen years to haul away the rubble of Berlin. But they were wrong; Berlin was rebuilt in just eight years."

"In the West, you asshole," says Pommerer. "We had to work and rebuild ten times longer than you. You got whatever they could give, we lost whatever they could take."

"Directly after the surrender," the voiceover continues, "the Soviets set busily to work filling all the important posts in the Eastern part of the ex-capital with Communists."

"What does he mean, Communists!" Pommerer breaks in. "They were looking for people with clean records. And most of the anti-fascists happened to be Communists."

I point out that Social Democrats and Christians also fought against fascism.

"Precisely—and the Soviets offered them jobs in the

bureaucracy, the schools, management; they begged them to participate. But there's one thing he didn't mention: in the 1946 Berlin elections, the Communists got twenty percent of the vote."

"Twenty percent isn't a majority."

"What do you mean, majority!"

"I mean you didn't choose communism."

"Just as much as you did your American democracy."

"But that only proves that neither system is home-grown German."

"True," says Pommerer. "But what was better for a people who elected Hitler in a landslide: imposed capitalism or imposed communism?"

■ It will take us longer to tear down the Wall in our heads than any wrecking company will need for the Wall we can see. Pommerer and I can dissociate ourselves from our states as much as we like, but we can't speak to each other without having our states speak for us. If I insist on majorities as instinctively as Pommerer distrusts them, it is because we have been equally receptive sons of the system that has brought us up. The possessive "yours" and "ours," "on our side" and "on your side" that creep into every German-German family reunion are not just a simple shorthand for the two states. They indicate a kind of belonging that transcends political options. The shorthand conceals a lesson preliminary to any exchange: only when both speakers have recited it can they begin to discuss the life that each still lives behind the Wall.

Two different wartime experiences: In 1945 Pommerer was living in Berlin, in Prenzlauer Berg. Down to the cellar every day during air raids, up to the kitchen for a half hour at noon to cook. His father had left a pistol behind in case the Russians came. His mother was supposed to kill herself and the children to save them all from rape. The Russians came on foot and with tanks. There were rapes, but not in his mother's house, not in their neighborhood. Other images remained: a Russian unties a farmer's cow and brings it to a German mother who can't nurse her newborn child. Slit-eyed Mongol subhumans cook for the vanquished, seat children on their tanks, and pass out candy. Pommerer's shame at the contempt of the defeated master race for the low-brow victors who don't know what to do with a light switch or a napkin. Fifteen thousand Russians died where the Soviet Memorial stands today.

In 1945 I was in Bavaria with my mother, fleeing from the Russians. The whistle of low-flying American planes; trains stopping in open country; rumors of five hundred dead bodies in the woods. The Americans arrived in planes. Later, jeeps drove into our Upper Bavarian village; they tossed sacks of sugar and groceries onto the street. Their clean, handsome uniforms, their bright faces, the casual posture of the soldier in the passenger seat who dangled his leg on the running board. Then the Care packages—turkey, salted butter, yellow cheese in cans. The Americans were luminous as gods, chewed something when they spoke, smoked and passed out cigarettes. They didn't rape; they had love affairs. They were rich, generous; they had white teeth.

The first English sentence Pommerer learned: Ami, go home.

My first English sentence: Have you chewing gum?

Thirty-five years later, these differences are the cornerstone of defense budgets. The experts' columns of figures on enemy nuclear firepower are haunted by the articles of faith we acquired in childhood: the Russians want to conquer the world. Or: the Russians know what war is like, and they want peace.

■ My aunt's house in Dresden stands on a wooded hill. Through the glass wall of the living room you can see an orchard sloping steeply down to the city. The interior decoration recalls a time when the West German middle class declared war on corners and edges and took their cue from English Chippendale: in the fifties, the "Now-we're-somebody-agains" of Frankfurt and Hamburg felt comfortable with ovals and kidney shapes. The three-story villa can accommodate the most elaborate life-style: this is private property of the sort the state allows its leading cadres.

Dora—as we have cautiously agreed I should call my aunt, whom I've never met before—has lived alone in the house since my uncle's death. She is a small, vivacious woman with sparkling eyes. She studies me, this stranger who introduces himself as her relative, and vainly searches for a feature she might recognize. With her cosmopolitan, Mediterranean air, she seems like a meteorite that has crashed from some mysterious distance into the Saxon minister's family that are my ancestors.

Why haven't I ever visited my aunt, why am I visiting her now? Little by little, when we've put the family silver down and the table has been cleared of Meissen china, names begin to surface—names for a buried part of the family history, but names, too, for its present amazing state. I faintly remember that it was neither partition nor the Wall that distanced me from the maternal side of my family. But my surprise stems from the recognition that I have once again encountered the privileged, upper-middle-class branch of my family here, in the poorer of the two Germanys. It seems clear that this branch has proved immune to the power of systems.

Unlike my mother, my uncle earnestly followed the path that lay open to the son of a Reichstag deputy from the German National People's Party. My mother incurred her father's wrath by falling in love with a choirmaster-organist and marrying far beneath her class, but her brother remained true to his origins and fulfilled everyone's expectations. He attended a polytechnic institute, became a mining engineer and later a mine executive. Because of his experience, and especially because he had invented a process for refining soft coal, he proved as indispensable to the Nazis as he did later to the Communists. He joined the National Socialists right after they came to power.

Following the collapse of the Hitler regime, he had to undergo a de-Nazification trial, but he was back at work within months. He stayed on in the Soviet zone and in 1948—here again at the forefront—he joined the East German Communist Party. He became director of various soft-coal trusts, won numerous honors, and lectured at a polytechnic. Since the new Party card—like the old Party card—was little more than a formality required for his work, he saw no reason to change his way of life. As he had before the war, my uncle spent his leisure time with friends of the family from banking, commercial, and industrial circles in West Berlin. No one would have thought of inconveniencing him by refusing him a visa. True, the systems had changed with the times, and occasionally a mild rumor of the Cold War must have reached the sailboat on which he and his friends spent their weekends, now in the East, now in the West. But the community of their success was stronger than any separation: now they were building the economy in two German states, not one, and they were still leaders. The gravitational pull of property and family determined which side they worked on more than any conviction did. They had attained a rank in their respective societies which showed political conviction to be what it probably always had been: a luxury of the underprivileged.

As this sketch materializes in my aunt's answers to my questions, my attention wanders more and more. Even during dinner I thought I heard footsteps upstairs, the closing of a door, the muffled voice of a TV announcer. All these noises sound as though they are supposed to be a secret. It seems someone is walking around on tiptoe, turning a doorknob very slowly, keeping the television sound at a whisper.

"Does someone else live here?" I ask finally.

My aunt looks at me, embarrassed. She has to apologize for her son's behavior, she says. It isn't dislike or

indifference that keeps him from welcoming his unknown Western cousin. Unfortunately for all of us, my
visit has come during his second year in the National
People's Army. Soldiers, like many of the higher cadres
in science, technology, and management, are forbidden
any Western contact. Permission can be obtained only
in exceptional cases and when a request has been sub-
mitted in plenty of time. Since I made my visit on such
short notice, her son wasn't able to postpone his week-
end furlough. So he has to offer me the rather unusual
company of a relative who is present only in the sounds
that he makes.

■ I had never heard before and haven't heard since about
this cousin. Since no one, other than an internalized
cop, could have prevented him from at least sticking
his head through the door, the "contact ban" by which
he voluntarily abided turns him into a fantasy double.

If I had grown up in the same circumstances, the same
house, the same town as this cousin, could I have been
brought to a comparable level of obedience? Do I imagine a flattering answer only because I've never been
subjected to the same pressure? Or would I have re-
belled precisely because of the pressure? If so, at what
point would I have started rebelling? When I was
drafted? During my civil defense training? Or even earlier, at the youth initiation ceremony when I turned
twelve?

If I had grown up in Dresden, in my aunt's house or

one like it, I would have ripped off Russian vodka rather than American cigarettes from the trucks of the occupation army. The first foreign words I learned would have been Russian, not English. I would have sung "The world needs you and you need the world, pioneer," instead of "Innsbruck, I must leave thee." I would have gone to Communist youth initiation rather than confirmation classes, would have watched Russian films about the Great Patriotic War instead of American westerns, would have become so fed up with the word "comrade" by age fifteen that I couldn't bring myself to say it at age twenty-five. I would have watched so many anti-fascist films, even as a child, that the American Holocaust series would have seemed merely tasteless. I would have read Nietzsche and Sartre in secret instead of Wilhelm Reich and Lenin, might for the first time have studied Marx of my own free will when I heard about the student movement in West Berlin.

And beyond that?

Would I still have practiced my violin while the others were playing soccer? Have preferred Spinoza to Karl May? Have heard that masturbation ruins your eyes? Have felt that silence at the table was worse than the bombs of World War II? Have heard in "Rock Around the Clock" the most important lesson since the Sermon on the Mount? Have learned Bob Dylan songs by heart?

If not, then I wouldn't be the same person.

But would I have turned out so differently that no one could recognize me? Where does the state end and a self begin?

We're somebody again. The "again" always bothered me in that phrase. If you finally become somebody, you must have been nobody once.

■ Pommerer responds to the story of my invisible relative in Dresden with: "So what? Don't you know that your soldiers can't use the transit highway to West Berlin? That they have to petition their superior officers when they want to travel into the DDR? That the border patrol reads every letter from West to East Germany?"

I didn't know it. I only know that we will fail in our attempt to cure the madness of one state by referring to the madness of the other.

I turned forty last year. The two states which bear the word "German" in their initials have just celebrated their thirtieth birthday. So I am ten years older than the state that has grown up around me and in me. On the basis of age alone, I can't call it my fatherland. What's more, this state represents only a part of the country that would be my fatherland. If my fatherland exists, it isn't a state, and the state of which I am a citizen is not a fatherland. If I respond to queries about my nationality by saying without hesitation that I'm German, I am clearly opting not for a state, but for a people that no longer has a state identity. At the same time, however, I assert that my national identity does not depend on either of the German states.

The same thing applies to the expression: "I come from Germany." Either it has no meaning, or I am speaking of a country that appears on no political map. By Germany I am referring neither to the DDR nor to the BRD but to a country which exists only in my memory or my imagination. If I were asked where it lies, I could only locate it in its history and in the language I speak.

If the Germans still have a fatherland, it survives mostly in the mother tongue; and if it is true that land comes from our father and language from our mother, then our maternal heritage has proved the stronger. In this respect the Germans seem to have returned to the beginnings of their history. After all, the word *deutsch* originally referred neither to a nation nor to a state; it meant "people," "of the people," and designated the common language of various tribes who had begun to assert their spoken tongue against the Latin of the bureaucracy and the Church. This linguistic unity existed for centuries before the founding of the Holy Roman Empire of the German Nation, and it has survived the rise and fall of all other unholy Reichs. Today the word "German" can be used without confusion only as an adjective, and even then with reference neither to a state nor to a fatherland, but—at least for the present—to a single noun: "language." And finally, as was the case a thousand years ago, the attempt to speak a common German language has to begin with a refusal to parrot the Church Latin of East and West.

■ "So keep it up and don't give in," I say as I leave, and wave my fist with my thumb erect in Pommerer's face.

"On Adenauerplatz," Pommerer answers, "I've heard there's a five-room apartment opening up. Could you look into it?"

"For you?"

"My exclusion from the writers' union is in the works. And I can imagine what will happen after that: I'll be writing for the drawer."

"You think they'll let you out?"

Pommerer shrugs.

"A writer? Anytime."

5

■ The evenings have grown cool now; at Charlie's they've brought the tables and chairs in from the street. I can see Robert's angular profile through the windowpane. But Robert doesn't seem to be expecting me; his glance briefly notes my entrance but hardly qualifies as a greeting. He has pulled his head down between his shoulders, the way he always does when he's trying to convince someone. A glass of mineral water and a cup of coffee stand before him. It is only when I round the giant papier-mâché bust by the counter—an unfortunate cross between Marx and Bakunin—that I see the person he's talking to.

To judge by her complexion, Lena has just returned from southern Italy. But what has brought her to this bar on Kurfürstendamm, where—and this used to say it all—only people like me pass the time? Once, from a distance, I pointed her out to Robert in a crowd, but I never told him her address or even her last name. In any case, there she sits behind a curtain of smoke, as beautiful and as stern as ever, in light Italian fabrics, not an excess ounce on her body, and so close to Robert you wouldn't think the table was big enough for six. She greets me without curiosity, a reunion tempered by suspicion. After all, why should she notice what I've learned on my trip, when we shared it only in my dreams? And why do I imagine I've gained insight about the two of us, something worth telling her?

I saw the lake, the town, the street where you lived. I went to the shop where for three years you . . . A cobblestone street, Lange Gasse, wasn't that the name? But what was it I wanted to say? It's true, people over there are different . . . Perhaps if you've grown up there, you can't ever be at home in the West . . . Anyway, I realized that you are still, yes, twenty years later . . . that clear, pure, frank quality . . . I mean, the reproachfulness, the need to place the blame outside you, to remain innocent . . . I only wanted to say, I won't apologize, justify myself anymore . . . Sure sure, I always had it better, all the little comforts, a child of the Marshall Plan . . .

But I won't, never again . . . I'm not going along with it anymore, the old you-demand-I-give; the incessant escalation of entry requirements, the bald-faced raising of the required currency exchange . . . I'm sorry, I like being able to drink a decent Italian wine again . . . I take back the "sorry" . . . Fine: I'll start by telling you how much money I earn, how much I pay in taxes, which car I'm going to buy next, what ruined fantasies, what impossible desires . . . it doesn't interest you . . . I only wanted to say: It's time you came out from behind your fence. You aren't a victim, you're an aggressor . . . just once I'd like . . .

"So this is your regular bar?" says Lena.

"What do you mean, regular bar?"

"Don't be so touchy!"

"Why? I mean: why not?"

"Is anything wrong?"

"No!"

"If something's up, you can always give me a call."

Robert has listened to us without expression; the sudden glow in his eyes seems meant for Lena, not for me. As Lena gets up and Robert hands her her bag, I catch an understanding in their glance that is older than words. Lena says goodbye, first to me, then to Robert and, without looking back, walks past the papier-mâché bust to the door.

"Why have you kept her hidden from me?" says Robert; and then, without wasting another word on Lena, orders a cup of coffee and a glass of mineral water. He looks at his watch, asks the bartender to turn up the sound on the TV, and moves his chair closer to the screen.

"We have to watch this. It's going to be exciting!"

■ The hockey game between the Soviet Union and the United States has just begun. It will be the last sporting event between the two countries until further notice: the U.S. has decided to boycott the Olympics in Moscow because of the Soviet troops in Afghanistan.

"The Americans, can you believe it?" says Robert. "They have it coming. Let them clear out of El Salvador first!"

The game is being played in the U.S.; the mood of the two governments has carried over to the players and the spectators. Every time the American team moves into the Russians' half, the spectators wave flags and hats in red, white, and blue.

"Those Western creeps with their flags!" Robert yells. "Hit 'em, Ivan, show those college boys!"

I see the goalie crouching in front of his goal in full armor. He has a helmet on his head, a wire mask across his face, heavy leather gloves on his hands, plastic shin guards on his legs; only when he crouches very low do his legs open a crack. Interstellar space is smaller than the cage behind him.

"Goal!" I scream.

"That wasn't a goal! It was a foul!"

Robert has sprung up in excitement.

"Didn't you see it? That Ami shoved the Russian

against the goalie . . . What? What's the referee saying? No foul?"

"The Russian fell against the goalie by himself!"

A brawl has started on the sidelines; five players, jammed into each other, fight with their bent lances for possession of the quick, invisible object; two players are pulling off their skates, wood is splintering, the referee calls it: "Goal!"

"I don't believe it!" Robert explodes. "Take a look, just take a look, the way the Ami hit the Russian—"

The instant replay shows it clearly: what to me is a point for the Americans, to Robert is a foul against the Russians.

■ The light in the courtyard isn't working. As I make my way between the garbage cans, I hear a voice from one corner. Gradually the outlines of the old man detach themselves from the darkness; he's fiddling with his door.

"Light, a light! Don't you have a light?"

I bring a flashlight from my apartment and shine it on Frieda Loch. This time she has on a curly black wig; rings and bracelets glimmer on her hands; the makeup from her last number has run down her face. Two enormous suitcases rest beside her. She stands on the mound of rubble in front of her apartment door and digs through her handbag in the dim glow of my flashlight. Makeup, silver comb, false lashes: she hunts and hunts and can't find her key.

"Maybe it got into one of your suitcases," I say. I help her open them: a snow-white gauze dress, a shimmering stole, fishnet stockings and garters, blonde, brunette, and auburn wigs, scarves embroidered in gold and silver, a Marlene Dietrich hat, an incredibly long, white lace veil. It all slowly sinks from the suitcases into the rubble, as though a treasure chest had sprung open. Frieda curses, goes over to the window, and pushes it inward.

"Could you . . . just a little . . . I'm not very heavy."

I grab the old man from behind and lift him onto the sill; he giggles lewdly. I can hear flowerpots smashing and glass breaking inside, and then the suggestive thanks of the old man, who leaves his rear end in my supporting hands longer than necessary. Did he just make up that story about having lost his key?

■ A new noise has drowned out all the other sounds in the building: the restorers are hammering at the plaster. They hammer away the bullet holes from the last war, the handsome bas reliefs that the weather has worked into the facades—a half-century of wall drawings.

"They don't stand a chance! Want to bet?"

"They've done it before."

"Not a chance! I'll bet you a case of beer!"

Through the half-open window I can hear the voices of two workers taking it easy on the scaffolding during their morning break. The plank they're sitting on runs level with the top of my window; I only see their four dangling legs.

"The DDR will be world champion in soccer at the next Olympics."

"Not a chance! I'll bet you a case of beer!"

"Okay, a case! They can do it, they go at it scientifically! Listen—you know Alex, my uncle's grandson over there? He has a classmate, she's an ace swimmer. She's two heads in the lead at the starting gun, I've seen it myself. Yeah, so they take someone like that out of school, she won't have to study Russian anymore, they give her a couple of shots and work her until she's as slippery as an eel. It's not pretty, but you get results."

"In swimming, sure—in swimming. Swimming is drill-work, and when you're talking drill, they can beat us. But soccer? Not a chance! You can't get anywhere by drilling—you need player personality, that's what, you need a feel for the ball, and you can't get that feel by drilling! You can teach a robot anything, but not that feel for the ball!"

"What's feeling got to do with it? Our players just aren't motivated anymore. They're ready to retire by the time they're in the regionals; they're already million-aires halfway up the ladder. They haven't got any steam —they're limp. The others, now—they're hungry. And when you're hungry, you go for it! You can see for yourself: on the horizontal bar, on the parallel bars, in ski jumping, javelin throwing, shotput, track—they're in the lead and we're back with the also-rans."

"Just wait until they've all got their VWs; then they won't run so fast."

"The Russians will make sure they don't all get VWs."

"Yeah, and the Russians will also make sure they don't come out world champs. The DDR coach will get a call from the Kremlin saying: 'Either you lose, or we're sending you to Siberia!' You've already lost your bet!"

"They'll do it—from hunger and science."

"They don't stand a chance. A case of champagne! They can take us in every other field maybe. But soccer? Not a chance!"

■ This time I'm the only entering traveler at the checkpoint on Heinrich Heine Strasse, but it takes longer than usual for them to call my number. They know me by now at customs; our greeting is friendly, almost casual.

"Nothing to declare? That's not nice of you. Your friends will be disappointed. Have I already asked you whether you're carrying any weapons, ammunition, printed matter, children—none of the above?"

"None of the above."

It seems I'm done; then, as though he were giving in to a sudden whim, the customs man motions me to pull over.

"Well then, let's get on with it," he says, pulls out a screwdriver, and sets to work. He starts with the hubcaps, takes off the wheels, carts the spare tire off for x-rays, shines a light through the trunk and on the motor. Then he moves to the passenger compartment: the floor mats, the metal plates under the floor mats, the lining of the doors, the leather upholstery on the seats. When he begins dismantling my stereo speakers, I abandon my principles and take the screwdriver out of his hand. In the next two hours we strip my Citroen down so thoroughly that we are left with an unrecognizable skeleton.

"What else do you do with your time? You're pretty handy with a screwdriver," the officer says.

"I write stories."

"What about?"

"About life; about you, for example."

"And can you make a living doing that?"

"I support myself with my screwdriver when I have to. How often do you actually find something?"

"Pretty often; when something's hidden, always."

"Hard to believe, given your methods. For example: If I had hashish on me, how could you find that with your screwdriver? Where are your dope dogs?"

"Dope dogs? What an idea! For that we have our nosy gnats."

"Nosy gnats? They fly away."

"Believe me—when we train gnats, they don't fly away. So, who are you going to see this time, if I may ask?"

"The Berliner Ensemble."

"Yeah, well I don't really care. Just making conversation. So you think I won't find anything with my methods? Okay, I don't want to brag. Maybe you do have something in your car anyway, and then you'll get a good laugh out of this afterward."

"I certainly would if I had anything in the car."

"What could it be?"

"Well, you and your screwdriver won't find it. And your nosy gnats won't, either."

"So what should I do? I'm always open to suggestions."

"You'd have to bring in a machine that reads minds."

"We've had that for years. Do you think it would be worth using on you?"

"I couldn't say."

"Me neither. But you make me wonder. What would I find inside your head?"

The officer asks me to follow him to the visa booth. Without a word he hands my passport back through the slit, refunds my visa fee and my road user's fee, changes my DDR money back into West marks, gives me all the receipts. We return to the car, and only then does he snap to attention and say in his official voice: "You have not been granted permission to enter the DDR. In accordance with international protocols, no information will be disclosed regarding the duration or grounds for this measure."

■ In the season when the shortest day of the year approaches and the branches of the chestnut trees begin to look like television antennae, I sometimes wake surrounded by blackness. The dream images I remember are about unexpected meetings, reciprocated glances, caresses without preparation or purpose. A gloss of harmony lies on them as it does on the pictures in a cigarette ad. At the moment of waking, I have a feeling of separation, violent, recent, as if a parting I always feared were now a fact, merely forgotten in the first hours of sleep. If I sit up then and switch on a light, everything is back in place. Through the wall I hear familiar breathing; there has been no fight, no departure is imminent. From the stairwell across the way I hear the sound of an elevator stopping; the refrigerator motor starts up in the kitchen; a last fly awakes and buzzes through the room. Nothing has ended. My black, laced shoes sit under the chair as they have for years—they will fall apart before I do. The blue shirt on the back of the chair has lasted longer than my last love, but the collar is beginning to show signs of wear. My portable typewriter has outlived the leaflets I typed on it, and the guitar on the wall will probably outlive me—I stopped playing it long ago. All in all, I'm one of the more durable things here. But the city outside, with its fire walls, garden walls, border walls—those walls will still be standing when no one is left to move beyond them.

ABOUT THE AUTHOR

Peter Schneider, born in 1940, has lived in West Berlin

since 1961. With his first novel, he became the spokesman

for a whole generation of young Germans. Political

journalist and essayist, Schneider also wrote the

screenplay for the internationally praised film Knife in

the Head. The Wall Jumper *is his first novel to be*

published in America.